Dino Vicelli

Private Eye
in a
World of Evils

Lori Weiner

ISBN 978-1-950818-75-4 (paperback)

Rushmore Press LLC
1 888 733 9607
www.rushmorepress.com

Printed in the United States of America

DEDICATION PAGE

Thank you to my wonderful, supportive husband Martin for his encouragement and to my daughter Kandice. I am grateful as well to my mother Alma, who led me to the inspiration of my life, the Holy Spirit. God does have a sense of humor. He created Dino, who was the inspiration for this book.

Contents

Preface...7
Chapter One 9
Chapter Two 16
Chapter Three 21
Chapter Four..27
Chapter Five...35
Chapter Six 44
Chapter Seven 50
Chapter Eight 53
Chapter Nine 60
Chapter Ten 64
Chapter Eleven...70
Chapter Twelve 77
Chapter Thirteen..84
Chapter Fourteen 88
Chapter Fifteen 98

PREFACE

The smell of pine was in the air as he slowly opened his eyes to pitch black surroundings. He gasped for air, wondering where he was. He lay there for a moment, remembering that he had been wandering down a dimly lit street through the fog. That is all he could remember.

He felt a sharp throbbing pain in the back of his neck as though his head were about to blow off of his shoulders. As he reached for the back of his neck, his elbow hit something. He reached into his pocket and pulled out a book of matches, struck one, then realized that he was in a pine box. He couldn't move. He struggled for a moment, trying to push his way out, but the top of the box wouldn't budge.

"How did I get in here?" he thought. "They must have knocked me out and put me in here. Better yet, how do I get out of this one? Don't panic," he thought to himself. "With all of my days as a detective, I should be able to think of something."

The voices from above signaled what they had in store for Vicelli. Fear engulfed him as he lay there listening to the shoveling of dirt falling down on the box. He reflected back on the last two weeks of his life, wondering if anyone would ever find his body. Could they ever stop the doctor's insane plan to change and control human life as it now exists?

CHAPTER ONE

A man walking into a downtown building in the heart of New York City went up the elevator to the third floor, walked down a long corridor and stopped in front of a glass door that read:

DINO VICELLI
PRIVATE EYE
Will Snoop Out Anything
VICELLI & VICELLI

The man opened the door and walked in to find a strange-looking blue- gray dog with a cigar hanging from his mouth, his feet up on his desk while he stretched back in his chair, asking, "Are you lookin' for me?" His voice was very deep and raspy as the cigar jiggled around in his mouth.

The man was stunned, not expecting to find a cigar-smoking dog behind the desk. The man, looking at him in amazement, said, "Yes, I guess I am."

"Yeah, come in," said the dog. The air in the room was hot, humid, and full of thick cigar smoke, with the sound of traffic coming in through the open windows.

The man came in, finding his way through the stale gray smoke that lingered in the air. He sat down while studying this small thin-looking dog with a long nose, long legs and a white chest, almost like a tuxedo. He was an Italian greyhound. He wore black pin striped pants with suspenders and black hush puppies. The man thought the dog looked sharp for what he thought might be a typical shady detective.

Dino looked at him and said, "What do I call you? Ya gotta name?" His rough demeanor was a little surprising to the man.

"My name is Jim Barnes."

"Okay, Mr. Barnes, what can I do for you?" asked Dino.

"I noticed your sign reads, 'Vicelli & Vicelli'; do you have a partner?" "Now, Mr. Barnes, why would you ask that? Couldn't it be that I am just so good that I could do the work of two men? I am one of those Italian boys; I am bigger than I look," said Dino.

"Well, okay, whatever you say, Mr. Vicelli. I did not think of it that way."

Mr. Barnes thought he was a little strange; however, felt he should still tell him the reason for his visit.

"I will get right to the point. Mr. Vicelli, you have a good reputation for finding people, and this is why I am here. Three days ago, my wife disappeared without a trace."

Dino sat there, eyeing the tall man in his expensive dark blue suit, olive- colored skin, jet-black hair, with a very stuffy demeanor. Dino could not help but wonder from what snobby society group he came.

"Tell me your story, Mr. Barnes," said Dino.

The tears began to roll down Mr. Barnes's face as he choked up while speaking.

"My wife, well, three days ago called me from her office saying that she had to work late and would be home by 6:00. I got home at 8:00 and she was not home. When she was not home by 10:00, I really started to worry. I began calling her friends, and no one had even seen her that day. I called her office and there was no answer. You see, the thing about my wife is, when she says she is going to be at a certain place at a certain time, she is always very punctual. She never called, and now it has been three days."

"Mr. Barnes, do you expect any foul play here? Does your wife have any lovers? You know, anything like that?"

"Mr. Vicelli, my wife is a very faithful, devoted person, she would never dream..."

"Yeah, yeah," Dino interrupted, "they all think the same thing of their wives. Does it ever turn out to be true?"

"Well, may I continue?" Mr. Barnes asked. "Of course," said Dino.

"Well, anyway, this is totally out of character for her. She is always home when she says she will be," said Barnes.

"Did you file a police report?" Dino asked.

"Yes, I did, but I do not think that they can help me as you can," said Barnes.

Dino began coughing and choking from the cigar hanging from his mouth.

Mr. Barnes asked, "Are you all right?"

"Sure, it happens all the time," said Vicelli.

"You should really consider stopping smoking," said Barnes. Dino just sneered at him.

"Well, I'll tell you what, Mr. Barnes, why don't you provide me with a list of your wife's friends and phone numbers and places she frequented, and I can start to work on it."

Mr. Barnes got up and walked over to Dino, extending his hand to shake Dino's hand, saying, "Thank you for your time, Mr. Vicelli." As Dino went to shake his hand, his cigar fell out of his mouth onto the floor.

"Ahh, I hate when that happens," said Dino. He bent down to pick up the cigar and noticed a drop of dried blood on Barnes's shoe. He acted very nonchalant and sat up, putting the cigar back in his mouth, not saying a word about it.

"Well, as I said, send me the info that I asked for and I'll see what I can do," said Dino.

Mr. Barnes turned and left. Dino just sat there, wondering who this man really was, and whose blood was on his shoe. He found this case very intriguing.

Dino decided to stop for the day and to head on over to Humberto's bar and grill, a small local hangout he had been frequenting for years. At the bar was a cute little Chinese Crested barmaid, whose name was Lackahair and whom he liked very much.

She had just started working there a month ago, and he always looked forward to seeing her.

He walked through the front doors of the bar, and there were all the regulars sitting on the barstools: Shelly the Schnauzer, who was a total lush, and Terry the Terrier, who tore up anything that was put in front of him because he was just a nervous type of guy.

Dino walked over, sat on the barstool, and saw Lackahair waiting on the customers at the other end of the bar. Then he looked over at the pool table, and there was Barry the Bullmastiff and Bernie the Saint Bernard playing pool. It looked like a friendly sort of game.

Dino got Lackahair's attention and waved her down to his end. She looked down at Dino. He could see how excited she was to see him. Her face lit up like the moon beaming off the ocean in the dead of night. She moved quickly down to see Dino.

"I am so glad to see you, I was not sure if you were coming in," she said.

"Oh, I wouldn't miss seeing you for anything in the world, doll face," he said. He reached into his pocket and took out a cigar, and she quickly jumped at the chance to light it for him.

"I missed you, Dino," she said as she lit his cigar, staring into his beady little eyes.

"You too, doll face, just got busy and cannot always find the time to come in. Why don't you get me a beer, doll face?" Dino said.

"Why, of course," said Lackahair.

There was loud yelling from the pool table. It was Bernie and Barry arguing about a wrong play on the table. The argument began to heat up as Bernie lifted the cue stick above his head as though he was ready to hit Barry with it. Just then the kitchen doors flew open, and the owner, a little Chihuahua with a large sombrero on his head, yelled at the top of his lungs, "Hey, you boys had better get out of here, I don't need this trouble in my place. You go now, leave, vamoose."

Barry and Bernie decided to leave, while giving each other a disgusted look. The little Chihuahua, Humberto, walked passed Dino. "Hey, Mr. Private Eye, how are you doing?"

"Good," said Dino. "Looks like you had a little trouble there."

"You know, Mr. Dino, it's not the first time it's happened between them two. I almost wish they would stay out of here; it is quieter without them. I don't need their business that bad," said Humberto.

Dino went back to focusing his attention on the little barmaid, Lackahair. He loved the way her eyelashes would flutter as she gazed into his eyes, and to feel her skin was like running his fingers through the fleece of a lamb, smooth and soft. He loved to touch her skin while she leaned on the bar when talking to him.

*　　*　　*

The next morning, Dino walked to the subway as he pushed and shoved his way through the crowded streets of New York. While walking down Fifth Avenue to his office, he picked up a newspaper from the local paper vendor by the name of Dave, who was a short blond heavy fellow with glasses. "Hey, Vicelli, how you doin' this morning?"

"Good," said Dino, as he handed him the money for his paper.

"Have a good one," said Dave. Dino looked at the paper, and there on the front page the headline read, *"Beautiful blonde missing from her Hillsboro home."* Under the headline, there was a picture of Katy Barnes.

Dino was stunned; he didn't realize that this would make the papers so quickly. He opened the front door to the office building and passed the guard at the front desk.

The guard yelled out, "Good morning, Mr. Vicelli."

"Good morning, Stan," Dino replied. Dino made his way into the elevator and pushed the fifth floor button.

He walked down the hallway and unlocked the door to his office, noticing a large manila envelope on the floor underneath the door. He picked it up and smelled the strong scent of perfume. He sat down at his desk, opened the envelope, and there were many photographs of Mr. Barnes with many different women at different places. He questioned why Mr. Barnes had neglected to tell him of his escapades with other women. Could he have maybe murdered his wife for some frivolous affair? Vicelli thought. Maybe Barnes came into his office to hire him just to throw him off the track. That would explain the blood on his shoe. Many questions were racing through Dino's mind.

He looked further into the envelope and found a note that read:

"Mr. Vicelli, I know about Mr. Barnes coming into your office to hire you. I think that it would be a serious mistake if you took his case. Mrs. Barnes disappeared two weeks ago. I believe that he could possibly have killed his wife. I don't know what he told you, but he is not the man that he appears to be. I knew Mrs. Barnes very well and knew of her troubling situation with her husband."

Dior Violet
PRIVATE EYE

CHAPTER TWO

He stretched out in his big co wqamfortable chair, resting his legs on the desktop and lighting a cigar.

His eyes gazed up at the silhouette through the glass door. There stood a tall, very curvy creature. The door flew open, and there was the most beautiful pair of legs he had ever seen. His eyes slowly moved up her long, tall, slender body, from the tip of her toes to the top of her beautiful head. He looked at her silky, long blonde hair flowing around her graceful, swanlike long neck. He noticed the diamond necklace draping around her neck, glimmering so brightly as the reflection of the stones danced on the wall. "WOW!" he thought to himself. "This is the most beautiful specimen of an Afghan I have ever seen." He was-n't able to take his eyes off of her.

She stood there with her hand on her sensuous, curvy hip. She spoke as he sat there in awe.

"Maybe I have the wrong place; she said your sign reads Dino Vicelli. Are you Mr. Vicelli?" Her voice was so soft and sexy with a very heavy southern drawl. "Mr Vicelli?" she asked.

Dino opened his mouth to speak. He felt as though his tongue were stuck to the roof of his mouth. The drool began to run down his chin.

"What's wrong, cat got your tongue?" she asked.

"Ahh, yeah, that's me, no, we don't have any cats here, I mean, ahh, I am Dino Vicelli." She rather chuckled to herself at his stuttering. "What can I do for you, ma'am?" he asked.

"Well, you can start by putting out that nasty cigar; my little lungs just can't handle it. Why, darling, you can't even see in here through this heavy cloud of smoke. If it weren't for those big, handsome dark eyes of yours, I wouldn't be able to find you," she said.

"What is your name?" Dino asked. "Why, it's Jezebel. People call me Jez."

She walked in and over to Dino and took the cigar from his mouth and put it out in the ashtray. "There, now maybe we can get down to business."

He jumped up and said, "Let me get you a chair."

"My, what a gentleman you are," she said.

"Now, ahh, Miss Jezebel, what can I possibly do for you?"

"I am the one who delivered that envelope that is on your desk. I was here earlier before you arrived and didn't know what time you get in, so I decided to leave it under your door. Then I came back to make sure that you received it," said Jezebel.

"Oh, that was the strong scent of perfume that I smelled lingering through the hallway," said Dino.

"I work for the greyhound people track, "Footprint Downs." I am a secretary there for a man by the name of Mr. Tyson."

Dino interrupted her, "Isn't there a lot of people abuse there?"

"Yes, well, I am not supposed to tell you this, but I think there is. They keep those runners in cages, two and three in a cage sometimes. I know they don't feed them very much, probably just enough to keep up their strength. They try to cut down on the cost of food, so the track can make more money on those poor people."

"However, that is not why I'm here. The envelope was from my boss, Mr. Tyson. He asked that I deliver it directly to you," said Jezebel.

"Well, what does Mr. Tyson have to do with Mr. and Mrs. Barnes? I read the strange letter with no signature. Are you telling me that the letter is from your boss?" said Dino.

"Mrs. Barnes worked for Mr. Tyson for many years; she was my predecessor. Between you and me, I believe Mrs. Barnes and Mr. Tyson were having an affair. I think that he was very much in love with her.

"Mr. Barnes has been coming into the office every day harassing Mr. Tyson, questioning him about the disappearance of his wife. I think he must have known about the affair. Finally one day Mr. Tyson called security, and they won't even let him in to the racetrack. There are many strange things going on there lately," she said.

"Like what?" Dino asked.

"Well, for instance, about six months ago, one of the boys that worked in the ticket office just vanished... It wasn't like him at all, because if he were leaving, I know he would have mentioned it to me. We always talked, he was a good old greyhound boy who never caused anyone harm. He would always show up for work, even when he was sick.

"There were a few times when I spoke to him that he sounded like he wanted to tell me something, but I never pried. He really sounded like he knew something, but was afraid. There are very peculiar things going on at the track lately. I was hoping that maybe you could help me find my friend and find out just what is actually happening there," said Jezebel.

She then took out her mirror from her purse and powdered her nose. "Something just doesn't feel right. My boss would just kill me if he knew I were here confiding in you," she said.

"Tell me something, was there a missing persons report filed on your friend?" Dino asked.

"Not that I know of. My boss told me that Gerard, that was his name, took a long vacation in Mexico. Mr. Tyson didn't seem very concerned," said Jezebel.

Now Dino was very confused. He sat there in deep thought. He needed to talk to Mr. Barnes. "What was the real connection?"

"Mr. Vicelli, are you still with me?" Jezebel asked. "Oh, yeah, yes, I am listening," he said.

"You look like you're a million miles away," she said. "No, I just have many unanswered questions." said Dino.

"Well, I think that is all the information I can give you right now," she said. She slowly uncrossed her legs, as his gaze was upon her long legs. She got up and said, "Well, Mr. Vicelli, it was a pleasure, but I must be running along now."

"What is your hurry? Maybe you would like to have dinner with me tonight. Then we could discuss this a little further," he said.

"No, I'm busy tonight, maybe some other time," she said.

She turned as he watched her walk to the door with each slow, sexy step that she took. "I'll be in touch, handsome," she said.

Dino sat and watched the door close behind her. He could feel the beating of his heart throbbing through his chest. The image of the tall, beautiful blonde would continue to linger in his head.

With his feet still propped up on the desk, leaning back in his chair, he closed his eyes and fell asleep. He began to snore so loudly that he was heard two offices down the hall.

Then a loud yelling woke him up. "Hey, Vicelli, knock it off. We're trying to work around here," as they laughed. Then the phone rang. He picked it up, saying: "Vicelli here."

"Mr. Vicelli, this is Mr. Barnes."

"Yeah, Barnes, been waiting to hear from you. I need to talk to you," said Dino.

"Oh, if it's about getting the information to you about my wife, I planned on doing that today. I will bring it to your office. I think you will have everything that you need from me then," said Barnes.

"Yeah, Barnes, except for payment. My fee is thirty dollars per day plus expenses and meals," said Dino.

"Oh. I guess we didn't discuss your fee. Well, that is acceptable. I will send you a check tomorrow," said Barnes.

"By the way, Barnes, you didn't tell me that your wife worked at the racetrack," said Dino.

"No, I guess I didn't, just slipped my mind," said Barnes.

"Did your wife have any type of gambling problems? I mean that since she worked there, the temptation would be great," said Dino.

"Not really, she never had any problem that I was aware of," said Barnes. "Do you want to tell me again just how long your wife has been missing?" asked Dino.

"I thought we already went through this, Vicelli. I told you that she had been missing for three days. Now why the strange questioning?" asked Barnes.

"Well, maybe I will pay a little visit to the track. Try my luck out," said Dino.

2
3

CHAPTER THREE

When Dino hung up the phone, he decided to head on over to the racetrack. He walked out the door and down the hall. As he was walking, he heard laughter coming from the offices down the hall. "Hey, Vicelli," they said, "why don't you put a cork in it when you doze off like that?" He knew they were looking for trouble by making fun of him. They were two very overweight accountants who never cared for Dino, and Dino, never thought too much of them.

He walked into their office, seeing one of the men sitting on the sofa and the other on the edge of his desk. The one sitting on the edge of the desk was smoking a cigarette. The man on the sofa said, "Come on in, Vicelli, and take a snooze," as they chuckled.

Dino walked over to the man with the cigarette, took it out of his mouth, and dropped the ashes on his shoe.

"Ya think I'm funny, ha? Makin' fun of me, are ya?" Dino said.

"Wait a minute, Vicelli, we're just having some fun with you," said the man on the sofa.

"You think I got a problem snoring, you guys got an eating problem. Look at your own problem and get off my back," said Dino. Dino turned and walked out the door and heard them quietly snickering behind his back.

"Yes, sir," they sarcastically said.

He walked out mumbling, "Boneheads."

He took the subway that dropped him off at the racetrack. He looked up at the sign that read, "Footprint Downs People Track." It was very crowded with people and dogs going to place their bets.

The third race was about to begin. He picked up a program to see who was running. He liked the favorite, *Gumshoe,* who had many wins. He walked over to the betting window and glanced down at all the windows in a row, and every clerk looked the same. All of them were black greyhounds wearing white visors that read, "Footprint Downs." They all looked identical with a white symbol in the shape of a star stamped on their forehead, right between their eyes. He wondered how they all could look so much alike.

He got up to the front of his line and said, "I want to place a fifty-dollar bet on number five, *Gumshoe,* to win." As he gave the clerk the fifty-dollar bill, he took a puff on his cigar and blew a big whiff of smoke in the clerk's face.

"Hey, put that thing out," yelled the clerk.

"Well, just give me my ticket and I'll get out of your hair," said Dino.

The clerk gave him his betting ticket, and Dino went over and sat down on the benches. Dino figured that if he hung around a while, he just might find a clue to all this; and besides, just maybe he would get lucky on his bets.

As he was sitting there, he looked over and saw her, the beautiful blonde who had been in his office, Jezebel. She didn't see him, but was walking toward the executive offices in the building.

He began to make his way over to her, waving his arms, trying to get her attention. He yelled, "Jezebel," but she couldn't hear him through the noisy crowd.

As he approached the building, she had already gone through the locked employee door. He tried the door, but it would not open. He made his way back to his seat.

The announcer then came on and said, "The flag is up, and away they go."

He watched the people runners break from the starting gate. Jezebel was right. They were very thin, gaunt-looking people with very long legs. Their ribs were protruding. They were all tall people with red shorts and T-shirts with greyhounds printed on the front of their shirts. They were moving fast, very fast.

The announcer was rambling, "And there is *City Slicker* on the stretch, and alongside is *Country Boy* running hard and fast, and in 3rd place is *Gumshoe,* and there is the long shot *Mudslinger* coming up from behind. He is coming up, he is moving up fast, he is along the rail, and he is neck and neck with *Gumshoe*, and the winner is *Mudslinger* by a nose."

Dino looked up at the large TV screen, watching the replay. He noticed that all of the runners had a black symbol in the shape of a star stamped on their foreheads. He wondered what this signified. Dino grumbled to himself, "Gumshoe should have had it, stupid race."

He flipped his program to look at the next race. He noticed there was a racer owned by Tyson by the name of *One to Clone*. He thought this to be very odd. The racer was a long shot and had not done very well in the past.

He was getting up to place another bet, when all of a sudden a loud gunshot echoed through the entire betting area and out through the bleachers. Panic set in, and people began screaming and running everywhere. There was so much chaos that he couldn't make out what was going on. He started walking toward the office doors and noticed a man standing there holding his stomach, bleeding. Dino watched him stagger to the ground.

Dino began yelling, "Someone get help, call for an ambulance." Dino ran over to the man, bent down and propped the man's head up in his hands.

"Hold on, pal, you'll make it."

The man looked up at Dino and with a very weak voice said, "I know who you are, watch out for Barnes."

Every breath the man took was an effort. "What? Save your strength, pal, you are gonna need it."

The man motioned for Dino to come closer. He whispered, "I don't think I'm going to make it, but look for the star."

"What star?" Dino asked.

His last breath whispered, "Keep searching, you'll find out. It could be mankind's last hope."

As the man died in Dino's hands, he looked up and saw in the midst of the crowd, the blonde Afghan. She turned and began to run.

Dino yelled, "Jezebel, come back. I need to talk to you."

The police pushed their way through the crowd. "Okay, let's break it up. Did anyone see anything?" they asked. The bystanders in the crowd all pointed to Dino.

"Did you see what happened, sir?"

"Well, ya know, quite frankly, no I didn't. I was just sitting here minding my own business playing the races, and then I heard all the commotion. That is when I heard the sounds of a gunshot. I saw him standing there bleeding. I just rushed over to help the poor guy out. By the way, I am a private detective. My name is Dino Vicelli. Poor slob, do you know who he was?" asked Dino.

"Yes," said the officer. "We already questioned a couple of people in the crowd, and it turns out his name is Tyson. He managed this track. Somebody just had it in for him."

Dino could feel the blood draining from his face. Dino thought to himself that the dying man he was holding may have been the key to this whole mystery.

"Did you know the man, sir? You look a little pale."

Dino replied, "No, but I am going to find out what happened here today." The death of Tyson was a great disappointment to Dino, as he never got a chance to question him about what he thought really happened. "What did he mean by the star, and what did he mean by mankind's last hope?" The questions were swimming about his head.

He left the track and hailed down a cab. He reached in his pocket and lit a cigar, and the driver turned and said, "Hey, buddy, you can't smoke that thing in this cab."

"Why not, my cigars go wherever I do," Dino said.

The driver slammed on the brakes and said, "Can't you read the sign posted on the back of the seat?"

"Alright, yeah, 'NO SMOKING,' got your point," said Dino as he threw his cigar out the window. "I got your point, just take me to Forty-Second and Madison."

The traffic was heavy, and the sound of horns blowing and tempers flaring was coming in loudly through the open windows of the cab.

Dino began to daydream about the beautiful blonde who was in his office and wondered how she fit into this puzzle.

"Hey, pal, are you going to tell me where you want me to drop you off?" "Oh, yeah, yeah, ahh, just drop me off at the corner here." He was only a couple of blocks from the office and decided that the walk would do him good.

"That will be seven dollars."

Dino pulled out a ten-dollar bill. "Keep the change."

He got out of the cab and began to walk. The weather was changing quite quickly from the hot, stale summer days to the bittersweet cold that was moving in. He could feel the cold air stinging his long nose. He remembered that he had ordered a nice box of Cubans from "Bud's Smoke Shop," so he decided to stop in.

There was Bud, a hefty little bulldog with a long cigar dangling from his mouth. In his deep, raspy voice, he said, "Hey, Vicelli, how ya doin'?"

"Okay, Bud, wanted to find out if my cigars were in," said Dino.

"Oh, yeah, they're in. Haven't seen ya lately, Vicelli, where ya been hangin' out?" asked Bud.

"I have been busy on a case," said Dino. "I hope a good one," said Bud.

"Don't know yet."

"Went into Humberto's and Lackahair was asking about you. I think she kind of likes you," said Bud.

"Yeah, she's a sexy little thing, but I just don't have the time right now," said Dino.

"There they are, need to get a ladder to reach them. They are up on the top shelf."

As Bud stepped up onto the ladder, a loud crash came through the window. He turned around to see a bullet coming right at him; before he could duck, he felt a swishing past his ear. He looked up at the cigar boxes on the shelves and saw a hole in one of the boxes.

"What the heck?" screamed Bud.

"Get down," yelled Dino frantically as more bullets were fired through the window. Bud fell to the floor behind the counter. Dino crouched down, crawling to get out of plain sight, crawling to where Bud was.

"Who's after you, Vicelli?" yelled Bud. The bullets were flying in, destroying the whole shop. They felt the sharp fragments of glass penetrating their skin. Cigar boxes began falling off the shelves. Bud was yelling, "Hey, they're destroying my place here, Vicelli, this place is all I got."

Then the bullets stopped. They both got up very slowly, putting their hands on top of the counter, peering out into the street through the holes in the glass window. They stood up and looked around at the mess that surrounded them.

Bud began mumbling to himself and snorting. It sounded to Dino as if Bud was on the verge of tears.

"Thanks, Vicelli, you brought all this trouble into my shop. It will never be the same," cried Bud.

"Sorry, Bud, I don't know who did this," said Dino.

"Maybe you should buy your cigars somewhere else," said Bud. "I'll get to the bottom of this, Bud," said Dino.

Dino laid a fifty-dollar bill on the counter and picked up his box of cigars (filled with holes) and walked out quickly.

"I will make it up to you, Bud," said Dino.

Just as he got out the door, the police were walking in.

"You again, every time there's trouble, we find you," said the officer. "Oh, you were the same cops at the track," said Dino.

"You really get around, Vicelli, don't you?"

"Look, I have to go. Can I answer your questions later? My friend Bud is in there, and he will tell you what happened. Besides, I don't have a clue as to who did this," said Dino.

CHAPTER FOUR

Vicelli ran quickly down the crowded New York streets to his Fifth Avenue office building. As he approached his office, he noticed that his door had been unlocked and left slightly ajar. He remembered locking the door.

He cautiously walked in, noticing the smell of a strong medicinal odor that engulfed his senses as he saw a hand coming from behind in front of his face. The cloth was getting closer to his nose. He fought to pull the hand away from his face, but it was too late, as he fell to the floor unconscious.

He lay there for what felt like hours, slowly opening his eyes. His eyes were fixed on the floor. He felt very groggy and unable to move. He looked over and saw those beautiful legs that he remembered from before. He smelled the scent of her perfume that lingered from her fur. His eyes crept up her legs as he heard "hello, darlin'." It was Jezebel.

"What are you doin' here? Did you have something to do with this?" Vicelli asked.

"Why, whatever are you talking about? Why would I be standin' here if I did this? I came in and there you were, out cold. I could not figure out what happened to you. For all I knew, you had too much to drink and passed out on the floor. I have been waitin' for you to open those gorgeous dark eyes of yours," said Jezebel.

"You've got some explaining to do," said Vicelli.

"Why, whatever do you mean, sugarplum, here give me your hand and let me help you up," said Jezebel.

"I can do it myself," he said as he pulled away from her. He got up off the floor and slowly walked over to his desk to sit down while holding his head. Jezebel walked behind him and said, "Let me help you."

She began rubbing his neck.

He quickly pulled away from her. "Cut the sweetness act out, sister, I want some answers.

"Why did you conveniently walk into my office at this time? Why did you leave the scene so fast at the racetrack when Tyson was murdered? What do you have to hide?"

Jezebel, frightened by Vicelli's anger, became very silent and began to sob. The tears ran down her face. "I had nothing to do with all of this. I only worked for Mr. Tyson.

"Well, I know he was involved in something big and shady. He tried to keep everything a secret, but you know, I screened all of his calls, and remember I told you there was something strange happening at the track with the disappearance of my friend? And now the death of my boss. I have a feeling that he knew about Gerard and where he really is now, which he is probably dead.

"It all started this morning when I put a phone call through to Mr. Tyson from Dr. Senrab. Mr. Tyson used to have me type letters to him, so I know of him and that he is a doctor of science. Anyway, I noticed that they were on the phone for quite a while, then I heard Mr. Tyson yelling at him, saying I can't do that, his voice got louder and louder. Then he slammed down the phone as though he were very angry about something."

Vicelli listened intently while reaching for a cigar in the box riddled with holes. He lit the cigar and Jezebel began to cough. "Do you have to light that thing?"

"I'm callin the shots here, sister, just keep talking," he said.

"My!" she said. She walked around the room and opened another window.

"Well anyway, I left my office at about 11:00 A.M. and went to the ladies' room to get some coffee. When I came back about half an hour later, Mr. Tyson was gone. The thing that really frightened me was there were drops of blood on his carpet in his office. I didn't know what to think, it wasn't a lot of blood, I just imagined it could be that he cut his finger. I was very curious as to what happened, so I walked down to the next level.

"I followed the hallway toward the exit doors, and the blood on the floor got heavier. Then I opened the doors, and that is when I saw him standing there, holding the side of his stomach. I heard the shots and saw him fall to the ground.

"I did see the man that shot him. I think he saw me, that's why I ran. I was scared," said Jezebel.

"He must have been shot or stabbed before he left his office. Of course if he had been shot in the office, people would have heard the noise and come running. Maybe he was stabbed," said Vicelli.

"Well, someone wanted to make sure that he was dead, that's why they shot him after they saw him come out. However, the gunman looked right at me after he shot him. He knows that I saw his face," said Jezebel.

"What did he look like?" asked Vicelli.

"He was a tall man with red hair, dressed in a suit, a white suit. I am frightened. I don't know if they will come after me next," said Jezebel.

"Well, whoever it is is after me as well. I want to know who was in my office, if it wasn't you, and who tried to kill me at the cigar shop? They made a bullet-filled mess out of my box of Cubans," said Vicelli.

"What? Someone tried to kill you?" she asked.

"Yes, or they were trying to kill the guy I buy my cigars from, and I seriously doubt that. I have a feeling someone wants me off of this case," he said.

She came over and sat on his lap as she caressed his face. "Well, lambie pie, maybe we should go to dinner," she said.

Vicelli sat and looked at her. His angry facial expression began to soften. "Maybe you're right, let's have dinner."

"Sure, darling. Can you pick me up at, say, 6:00?" she asked. He looked at the big grandfather clock that stood against the wall, and it was now 3:05

P.M. This would give him a chance to close his eyes for a little shuteye after his exhausting day.

She gave him a big smooch on the cheek, leaving her red lipstick stain on his face. She wrote her address down, saying, "This is where you can find me." She got up and walked toward the door, saying, "See ya later, sugar." As she turned around, she caught him eyeing her, gave him that big, sweet charming smile and walked out the door. As he watched her, he seemed to forget all the chaos that had happened that day.

*　　*　　*

When he got home, he fell into a deep sleep and began to dream of a tall redheaded man in a white suit walking into his office, but the man had no face, and all he could see was the red hair. He looked at the man's shoes, covered in blood. The blonde then walked into his office and knelt down in front of the man and began wiping off his shoes. Then the man reached into his pocket, pulled out a gun, and pointed it at Vicelli's head. The blonde was laughing boisterously, throwing her head back as she laughed.

He woke himself up screaming as he heard a loud crash in the kitchen. He ran to the kitchen and noticed the window had fallen shut, and there on the countertop was the neighborhood cat, Hairy. "Oh, it's only you. I know what you want, I'll give you some milk," said Vicelli.

*　　*　　*

He walked up to Jezebel's front door and noticed it was partially open.

He walked through the door, saying, "Anyone home?"

"Hello, Jezebel, are you here?" No one answered. The house was very quiet. He looked around the living room and noticed a lamp that had been turned over, and also a broken vase with flowers lying on the floor. He walked into her kitchen, where bloody fingerprints stained the floors and the stove.

His heart started to race. The sickening feeling in the pit of his stomach overwhelmed him. The worst was going through his mind.

At this point, he wished he had taken the gun from his safe for his own protection.

He called out her name, walking to the open bedroom door, where the same bloody fingerprints were screaming the sign of murder across the door. The beige carpeting was covered in bloody footprints.

As he walked into the room, the bedroom door shut behind him. He couldn't believe his eyes. He walked over to her body, and her beautiful long blonde hair dangled over the edge of the bed.

There she was, lying sprawled out across the bed face down with a knife in her back. He sat down on the bed next to her, gently pushing the hair back from her face, and it was her, the sensuous blonde he came to take to dinner.

"Oh, Jez," he yelled. He felt her pulse and knew she was dead. By the looks of things, the stabbing took place in the kitchen, and then she must have dragged herself into the bedroom.

He felt panicked. He couldn't call the police, because then he would be at yet another murder scene. He was trying to think fast as to what he should do.

He sat there on the bed next to her, pausing, listening to the floorboards creaking.

"Who's there?" he said, then once again, "Hello, anyone there?" He was like a sitting duck. He ran and hid behind the door as he heard the chamber of the gun clicking as it was ready to fire. He watched the doorknob slowly rotate, and the door began to open. His heart was racing. Sweat was running from his brow as he felt the adrenaline race through his body. He watched the tall redheaded man walk slowly through the door. A revolver was in his hand, leading the way.

Vicelli looked over and saw a hat rack standing next to him. He knew he had to move quickly before the man turned around and found him standing behind the door. Just as the man began to turn around, Vicelli picked up the hat rack and swung hard, smashing him in the head. The gun fell to the floor, shooting up into the ceiling. The redheaded man slumped to the floor, unconscious.

Vicelli knew the stranger was out cold. He stepped over the body and quickly went over to Jezebel's dresser to look for any clues. As he was searching through her drawers, he came across a small white star necklace in a box full of jewelry. Strange, he thought, this is the same white star that Tyson mentioned before he died.

In the bottom drawer, he found a box of pictures. The pictures were of the missing Katy Barnes and a man that looked like her husband, Jim Barnes.

He went over to Jezebel's closet and began to thumb through her clothes, feeling the heart-wrenching sorrow as he clenched one of her dresses in his hands, laying his head against the dress, smelling the sweet smell of Jezebel. As he lifted his head, he looked down the rack and there was a familiar-looking dress. As he held up the picture to the dress, he saw the same dress that Katy Barnes wore at the luncheon. "How could they have the same dress?" he questioned. "Was it that much of a coincidence?" He thought to himself, there is nothing out of the ordinary about the picture itself. So Katy Barnes was at a luncheon for her boss, Bill Tyson. Nevertheless, the dress, how did Katy Barnes's dress get into Jezebel's closet?

A groaning was coming from the floor. The man was waking up. Dino quickly walked passed him and ran out the door.

He walked out the front door, looking around to make sure no one had noticed him. His walk was brisk down the street lined with elm trees. It was dusk now; the streetlamps were just beginning to come on.

"How did this happen?" he thought to himself. "Someone must have known that she came to see me. Why did they kill her? Did she know too much? What did this have to do with the tall redheaded man?" The questions were just spinning around in his head. He kept walking, not even noticing what time it was or how dark it was getting.

He found himself at his front doorstep. He poured himself a drink and plopped down on the couch. He stayed up most of the night, just sitting and thinking. His eyes shut for what seemed like only a couple of minutes, and then he opened his eyes to a long pistol staring him in the face.

He tried to get up. "Going somewhere, Vicelli?" Vicelli looked at him in amazement. It was Jim Barnes.

"What are you doing here, Barnes?" Dino asked.

"I forgot to bring the information by about my wife, but it does-n't look like I am going to need you on the case anymore.

"Vicelli, I could keep you on, but seeing that you don't believe a word I say, where is it going to get me? It's funny, I hire you and you believe the first jerk who comes along and tells lies about me, like Tyson. He was never any good, but you can't work for both of us," said Barnes.

"Barnes, in case you aren't aware, Tyson has been murdered," said Dino. "Really, I should pin a medal on whoever did it. He was a worthless human being. Do you have any idea how long he was seeing my wife behind my back?" said Barnes.

"No, I really don't. Is that why you killed her?" asked Dino.

Barnes put the gun right into Dino's forehead, "I ought to kill you right now. I have never committed murder, but if you don't believe me, you are not going to pin this on me. I can't let that happen. I just wanted to find out what happened to my wife," said Barnes.

Dino pulling the gun away from his forehead. "Wait a minute, buddy; let's try to be rational about this. I want to help you. As I said, Tyson is dead. I wasn't saying you killed him or her. But why don't you give me a chance to get to the bottom of this, give me some time," said Dino.

"Well, I want to know what you found out about my wife and Tyson. Look, Vicelli, I was in love with my wife, but never really had the time for her. Yes, I did have affairs; my wife was always at work with that bum. I think Tyson did away with her. I think they were having an affair. She worked for Tyson for years. She also knew a lot about his business and the track's business. Maybe there was foul play going on."

Barnes put the gun down, resting it by his side. "There were many times that she talked to me on the phone, saying that there were some peculiar things going on there. I know she appeared to be frightened at times. She could never come out and tell me what was actually happening there. I just want to find her," said Barnes.

Dino got up off the couch with a blanket wrapped around him and began to walk into his bedroom.

"If Tyson did kill your wife or has her tucked away somewhere, this is going to be a much tougher case to crack, now that he's gone. Excuse me, Barnes; I think I need to get dressed. Give me a minute and I'll be right out." Dino grabbed his boxer shorts while talking to Barnes from the bedroom, as he grabbed a cigar and lit it.

"So tell me, Barnes, were you hoping that I might be able to confirm your suspicions about your wife?" he yelled from the bedroom.

There was silence, and then he heard the front door slam. Dino went out into the living room and Barnes was gone.

CHAPTER FIVE

As he walked toward his office, someone yelled, "Hey, Vicelli, it looks as though someone really made a mess of your office last night. Could-n't help but notice, your door was wide open."

"What?" yelled Dino as he ran down the hallway to his office.

He walked in and saw the beautiful old grandfather clock smashed to pieces on the ground. Glass everywhere, papers all over the floor, books from the bookshelves scattered and piled high everywhere. There on the wall, someone had painted in big letters, "BACK OFF VICELLI!" A large white star was beside the letters. He climbed over the books, papers and glass, puffing on his cigar, saying to himself, "What to do with this mess, and what rotten son of a gun did this? In addition, what were they looking for?"

"Got your hands full, Vicelli?" one of the accountants from down the hall said.

Dino was silent.

The man walked away, snickering and saying, "Stupid dog."

Dino found his way to the chair and sat down, leaned back and put his feet up on the desk. In his desperation, he thought of Lackahair. He needed someone to help clean the mess. He remembered her sweet smile and charming way.

He decided to take a little trip down to Humberto's Bar and Grill. He closed his office door and left the mess. He got into a cab. "Do you know where Humberto's Bar and Grill is?"

"Yep," the driver said. To Dino's surprise, the driver was a greyhound, looking the same as the greyhounds from the track. Same star on his head, same visor and same look. Dino thought it very strange that they all looked alike, all black in color, same facial expressions, same features, and same symbol on the forehead.

"Hey, buddy, aren't you from the Footprint Downs People Track?" Dino asked.

"Yep, this is my moonlighting job. The track doesn't pay a whole heck of a lot," said the driver.

"Ahh, what's with the star on your forehead?" asked Dino.

"Don't know. When I first came in for the job, they told me that I needed some surgical work on my teeth. I went in for the surgery and when I woke up, I had this star on my forehead. They told me that the seal was mandatory to work at the track, but I never really questioned it. When I started the next day, everyone else had one, so I didn't ask any further questions."

"Do you know anything about the murder at the track the other day?" asked Dino.

"Why all the questions?" asked the driver. "Oh, just curious," said Dino.

"It sounds like you're writing a book. Are you a cop or something like that?" asked the driver.

"Yeah, something like that," said Dino. "Did you know the man murdered there the other day?"

"Yeah," said the driver, "he was the manager, nice guy but a little strange, didn't know too much about him. He was a friendly kind of guy, but he would walk past you and never look you in the eye. Almost like he felt guilty about something," said the driver.

"Really," said Dino.

"Well, buddy, here's your stop. The fare will be $5.20."

Dino walked into Humberto's, and there was the same old crowd. The pool hustlers were back, Barry and Bernie. Then he heard this deep little voice saying, "Hey, Vicelli, how's it going?" He turned around and looked down and there was Humberto, welcoming him with a big smile.

"Good, Humberto, very good," said Dino.

Dino went to the end of the bar and sat down, and out from the kitchen came Lackahair. She looked at him with great excitement. "Would you like a beer?" she asked in her sweet little voice.

"Sure, and when you get a minute, I need to talk to you," said Dino. "Okay," she said as he watched her walk to the end of the bar. She brought him a beer.

"I need a favor from you, beautiful," said Dino. "Of course, Dino, anything for you," she said.

"Well, I got myself wrapped up in this strange case and it caused me some trouble. Would you consider coming back to my office and help me clean up a mess that someone made? They really thrashed the joint," said Dino.

"Really, are you in trouble?" she asked.

"Yeah." He reached into his pocket and lit a cigar.

He looked up to the sunlight catching his eyes as the front door opened, and then a silhouette appeared of a woman that had the same shapely body of Jezebel, walking through the front door with the tall redheaded man.

They walked over to the bar stools and sat down. Dino's mouth fell open and his cigar fell to the floor. He heard Lackahair say, "Are you all right? Dino, your cigar fell," as she rushed over to pick it up.

Dino couldn't take his eyes off of the couple that just came in. "Dino, Dino, here is your cigar," as she handed it to him.

He could only see her silhouette in the sunlight until the door started to close. His heart began to race while he thought, she isn't dead, it's her, or is it? What is she doing with the man who was in her house?

"Dino, do you know those people that just came in or what?" asked Lackahair.

"What people?" Dino asked.

"You know who I'm talking about. You're really staring at them," she said.

"No, no, don't believe I do," said Dino.

As the door closed, Dino could see that it wasn't Jezebel. However, it definitely was the man in Jezebel's house. The resemblance to both was uncanny.

"Well, anyway, if you're ready to pay a little attention to me, then I can finish telling you that I would be happy to help you anytime you need me to," she said.

He watched the two of them sitting there talking and noticed they kept staring at Lackahair. They called Lackahair over. The blonde dog ordered a glass of red wine, while the man seemed to be questioning Lackahair. Dino noticed how her hands delicately picked up the glass and put it to her lips. All of her very feminine actions reminded him of Jezebel. He wished that it was she and she were alive.

He watched as they finished their drink and left. All the while, Lackahair kept watching Dino. Dino got up, went to the front door, and looked outside to see if he could see them, but they were gone, out of sight.

He went back in and sat down. "What did they talk to you about?" he asked.

"Well, it was a little strange; the man was asking me if I work here full- time and what my hours are. I don't know why," she said.

"What time are you off tonight?"

"It's funny you should ask, I'm off in about 10 minutes," she said. "Good, I am taking you to a little French restaurant around the corner for dinner, and then maybe we could go back to my office and you could help me."

"I would love to. Who were those people?" she asked. "No one, someone I thought I knew."

She grabbed her coat and they left. They walked down the street arm and arm.

Dino had a very uneasy feeling, a feeling as though someone were watching them. He kept turning around, looking over his shoulder. "You're edgy tonight, Dino, what is wrong?" she asked.

Then she said, "Dino, there is something that I need to tell you." "What is it?" asked Dino.

"Well, I am not really a bartender," she said.

"What are you talking about, Lackahair, if you can bring me a beer, then I consider you a bartender," said Dino.

"I am not who you think I am. I can't blow my cover right now, but I believe that you are in real danger," she said.

"Explain, I don't know what you mean, are you working for the police?" asked Dino.

"Something like that," she said.

He looked back again and saw a police car following him. In the front seat was a pit bull wearing a police uniform, along with a balding man. Dino kept wondering why they were slowly following behind them. The streets at that time were empty, and they seemed to be the only car on the street.

Dino grabbed Lackahair by the arm. "We need to move a little faster." "Why?" she asked.

"Please just do as I say," he said.

The car pulled right up onto the sidewalk in front of them, blocking their way.

The two police got out of the car. "Are you Dino Vicelli?" "Yeah, I am, what about it?" asked Dino.

"I have to take you in for questioning," said the pit bull cop. "Why?" asked Dino.

"I think you know, pal."

"Wait a minute, officer, what is this all about? I work for the FBI and I can vouch for Mr. Vicelli," said Lackahair.

Then, suddenly, Dino pushed Lackahair aside and began to run.

They yelled, "Stop or we will shoot," and then they did shoot, as Dino wasn't stopping.

Dino yelled, "Lackahair, run and get out of there."

Dino ran and ran as fast as his soft sole shoes would carry him. He could hear Lackahair yelling, "Dino, where are you going and what's going on?" He jumped over some trash cans and climbed a chain link fence, which led to the next street.

Dino kept on running for blocks. Then he heard a car pull up beside him. "Vicelli, get in." He turned around and a black Jaguar convertible was moving alongside of him. "Vicelli, get in," she said. He looked and it was Jezebel. He quickly ran to the passenger side and jumped in. "Hold on," she said as she accelerated to 90 miles per hour.

She was driving recklessly and fast. "Whoa! Slow down." Putting on his seatbelt, he found himself clenching the armrest. "Do you mind telling me what is going on here?"

"Oh, sugar, just shut up and hold on, you're goin' for the ride of your life."

He said, "Yeah, I think I have been on one all along."

"The only thing we need to be doing is thinking about losing those cops now."

She looked in her rear view mirror, watching them behind her with their sirens wailing. She continued to drive fast while dodging in and out of traffic. She was like a racecar driver trying to win a race, although this was a race to the finish line for their lives.

She looked back again and saw the pit bull climbing out of the window. He climbed onto the hood of the police car while the car was moving. Dino turned around and said, "They're getting closer."

"Can you believe this cop; he is standing on the hood while the car is moving," she said.

"I know what he is doing; he is going to try to jump onto our car, and you have to move faster," Dino said.

"I can't, there are too many cars in front of us," said Jezebel.

All of a sudden, they heard a loud thump and turned around, and there on the trunk was the pit bull. They heard footsteps on the roof as he slid down her windshield. She began to weave the car from side to side, almost hitting cars on the side of her, trying to throw him off. He then reached around and grabbed on to the door handle, hanging there as the car was flying down the street. She opened the window and started banging on his hands, trying to pry him from the door handle.

"Hey," he was yelling, "I just want to talk to you."

"You can talk to the pavement, sir," she said. She approached an intersection, making a hard right as he went flying onto the street.

She looked into her rear view mirror and saw the police car stop and pick him up.

"We lost them, sugar," she said.

"Good, maybe we can slow down a little now," said Dino.

Now that he had a chance to take a deep breath, he looked over at those long slender thighs and the long eyelashes that used to flutter at him as she spoke. Her diamond star-studded necklace still caught his eye as he noticed the sparkling jewels glistening off the dashboard. Her scent lingered around his nose.

"Who was the dead dame on the bed?" he asked.

"That is why I am hiding. That was my roommate, Lou Labelle," she said.

"That was your roommate?" Dino asked.

"Yes, if you noticed, she looks very much like me." "Yeah, I'll say, just like your twin," said Dino.

"Well, there are noticeable differences if you really take the time to look. Whoever killed her thought it was me, obviously. I have been driving around looking for you, hoping that I would find you. I knew that you would find her because you were supposed to pick me up at

6:00. After I left your office today, I went home to change and I found her dead. I was so upset I didn't know what to do. I ran out of the house frantically. I was afraid to call the police. I think they may be involved in some way. I wasn't about to take a chance."

"There was a woman who came in who I thought could have been you, until I saw her in the light. I think I know who killed your roommate. Do you know a tall redheaded man?" asked Dino.

"That was the man who I saw standing with the gun in his hand that killed Mr. Tyson. That explains it; he must have thought Lou La-belle was me. Poor Lou Labelle, she lost her life for a case of mistaken identity," she said.

"It seems as though I am in real trouble with the police. I think that they think I killed you. You need to go to the police with me to tell them what happened," said Dino.

"I can't do that. How do you know that someone in the police department might not be in on this conspiracy? The killer thinks that he has already done away with me, and I want him to go right on thinking that."

"Jezebel you can't hide out forever." said Dino.

"I can, at least until this thing blows over and they catch this guy."

"The way I look at it is my life is on the line, and I could go to jail for a long time," said Dino.

"I'm not going to let that happen to you, sugar, we will work it out."

She looked at him, smiling with those pearly white canine teeth as she blinked her long eyelashes. "You can't resist me, can you?"

"What do you think? You saved my life," said Dino.

CHAPTER SIX

"Dino, I want to take you somewhere. Remember I told you about the doctor who always called Mr. Tyson? The last day that he was alive, he sounded very upset on the phone. That was after I put the call through from Dr. Senrab. I have a feeling that he may be at the bottom of this. Maybe we could sneak into his house and look around."

"Wait a minute," said Dino. "I can't do that. That is breaking and entering."

"I bet you could, you are a private detective, you are probably used to this kind of thing," said Jezebel.

She drove along the coast until she came to a dirt road, where she pulled over. The sounds of the ocean waves seemed to soothe the chaotic feelings they were having.

"Please do this for me. It's the house on the top of that hill."

They looked up and saw a massive house sitting on top of a bluff that looked over the ocean. From the front yard, a light reflected into the sky, which was in the shape of the star he had seen on the greyhound's forehead.

Dino yelled, "That's the star that Tyson was talking about."

"What are you talking about, Dino? That is the doctor's house," she said. "I am talking about the reflection of the star in the sky. Tyson told me to look for the star, before he died," said Dino. "What does that signify?" she asked.

"I don't know, but I need to find out," said Dino.

"I was there with my boss to get some papers signed about a week ago.

It's funny, I dreamed about this house long before I was ever there.

It looked so familiar to me, and I can't figure out why. I have been thinking about that conversation between Senrab and Tyson for days. It really bothered me, and then shortly afterward Tyson died. Don't you think that is a little odd?" she asked.

"Or maybe just a coincidence," said Dino.

"I doubt it. Anyway, will you do this for me?" she asked.

Dino looked at her, hesitating, but then couldn't resist those beautiful brown eyes gazing at him.

"Yes, I guess so," he said reluctantly. "Do you have a plan?"

"Yes, I will distract the guards and you go in through the back door," she said.

"What if the doctor comes in while I am there?"

"He won't, every Tuesday evening he has a Rotary dinner. My boss used to meet him there. I know he won't be home. Just be careful," she said.

They got out of the car and opened the hood. She pulled the ignition wire, so her car wouldn't start. They began to climb the hill while Jezebel was carrying her shoes in her hand. They got to where the back entrance was and looked through the chain link fence, watching the Doberman Pinscher guards, who were equipped with rifles, patrolling back and forth.

"There are only four guards," she said.

She picked up stones and threw them over the fence into some leaves, which made a rustling sound. The spotlights went on, and the guards yelled, "Who is there?"

Dino quickly and quietly ran over to the side gate as the guards were running toward Jezebel with their guns drawn.

"Hello, boys. Can you please help me?" she said.

They looked at the beautiful, seemingly helpless blonde standing there. "Help with what, ma'am?" asked a guard.

"Why, my little ol' car broke down over that hill and I just can't get it started. I would so much appreciate it if you big strong boys could help me."

"Well, sure ma'am, we would be glaaad to help," said the guards. "I knew I could count on you boys, you're all so sweet."

She turned around and walked in front of them as they watched the swaying of her hips. They started down the hill, when one guard said, "Ma'am, let me help you." He picked her up and threw her over his shoulder so she wouldn't hurt her feet on the rocks.

"Oh my, you are just too kind," she said.

Meanwhile, Dino's path was clear. He made it into the house. There were large picture windows that reflected the ocean's waves beneath. He noticed a black and white picture on the wall of the "Footprint Downs Race Track."

He tiptoed across the marble floors to a spiral staircase that led to the upstairs. After peeking in several doors, he found the master bedroom. He began searching through drawers, not really knowing what he was looking for. He made his way over to the closet, and as he opened the door, he saw a pair of shoes with blood on them. "That's strange," he thought, "they look like the shoes that Barnes was wearing when he came into his office. What are Barnes's shoes doing in this man's closet, if they are Barnes's shoes?" He took the shoes with him to test for DNA.

At the bottom of the stairs, he noticed a long hallway past the living room. He kept walking until he saw a set of locked double doors. A loud humming noise was coming from behind them; it sounded like machinery.

He heard the front door shut, footsteps coming down the hall and the voices of two men. He quickly ran down the hall to another room. This time the doors were unlocked. It was a large room with glass encasements hanging by chains from the ceiling. There were about 20 of them in a row. It was so cold that he could see the breath coming from his mouth. At the other end of the room was a kennel with many empty dog crates. He crawled quickly into an open crate.

"I took care of everyone just like you asked me to, Dr. Senrab." He could hear the voices but couldn't see the faces.

"Thank you, Ron, you're very competent."

Then there was silence. "Shhh!" he heard the one man say. "What?" asked the other.

"Are you sure they're all out of here? I could have sworn I heard a cage rattling."

"Yes, Doctor Senrab, I took care of them all personally." "Well, you had better check all the cages again."

"Yes, sir, I will. I just have to take care of one small matter first." The lights shut off, and there was silence once again.

Dino didn't realize it, but when he stuck his head out of the cage and then went back in, the cage had locked. He squeezed his finger through the cage, trying to turn the lock, but nothing was happening. He knew he had to get out of there before someone came back. He began rattling the cage very quietly, hoping to jar it loose. As he shook the cage door, he put his finger through and turned the lock and the door opened.

His heart was pounding from anxiety; his paws were wet with sweat. He had to get out of there quickly. He looked up at the top of the wall and saw a little vent window. There were crates piled up to the window. He stepped on one crate and then attempted to step on another. "Please help me," he heard.

Dino paused and looked into the crate. "Are you all right?" "No, please help me, I am wounded."

"Hold on there, pal, let me get you out of there." He opened the crate to a greyhound that looked very ill and very thin. He pulled him out and pushed through the window, throwing the shoes in his hands after him. He put his arm around the dog to help him walk.

He was hoping that Jezebel was still entertaining the guards while he made his escape.

Meanwhile, the guards were busy looking under the hood of Jezebel's car.

"Well, ma'am, why don't you get in the car and start her up."

She turned the key and the car started. "Oh, boys, you just saved my little life."

"Well, ma'am," he said, "it looks like your ignition wire was loose." "Thank you, boys," she said.

He shut the hood and said, "Well, we have to get back now." She knew that she had to stall them even longer as Dino wasn't back yet. She then dropped her keys in the grass, where it was very dark.

"Well, how clumsy am I ever? Did you boys see what I just did? I can't find my keys." The guards began hunting for her keys. Jezebel looked up and saw Dino and the greyhound standing on the hill. They hid behind a tree.

"Oh boys, boys, I see them, I see the keys. Thank you so much. You just run along now and do a good little job like you were before," as she blew them a kiss.

They climbed back up the hill, and Dino waited until they were out of sight. Dino and the greyhound climbed down the hill toward the car, slipped, and tumbled to the bottom. The greyhound yelled, "My leg."

"Shhh!" Dino said.

She ran over to them, grabbing Dino's arm, helping them both up.

"Who is this, Dino? You have some extra baggage here, darling. Whose shoes are you carrying?"

"I couldn't just leave him there; he is in a lot of pain. I think he needs a doctor."

The greyhound was moaning and groaning.

"Well, sugar, in case it didn't dawn on you, we only have a two seater car. Where do we put him?"

"We will scrunch him in the seat next to me," said Dino. "Did you get any evidence?" she asked.

"Yes, I did, these shoes. I am not sure, but I think they belong to Mr. Barnes. I am going to find out whose blood this is. I heard two people talking about if they got something out of somewhere. The conversation didn't make much sense. That place was strange. I was in a room where things were hanging from the ceiling. I don't know what they were used for, but it was odd."

"What kind of things?" asked Jez.

"I don't know, I really can't explain it," said Dino. "I wonder how the disappearance of Mrs. Barnes fits into all of this, or does it have anything to do with it at all?"

"I don't know, darlin', but I feel horrible that my roommate had to die. She was so sweet. We looked so much alike that I just know they thought it was me. I'm very scared right now, Dino."

"I know, Jez, we will get to the bottom of this," said Dino.

"Right now, I think we need to get this guy to the hospital. You know, he hasn't said much in the last 10 minutes, is he okay?" she asked.

"Hey buddy, are you okay?" As Dino shook him, he didn't move.

"Are you okay?" Dino asked. "Jezebel, stop the car. I think this guy has either passed out or isn't breathing."

Jezebel, pulled over to the side of the road. She felt his pulse. "Dino, he is dead."

"Oh no, I didn't think there was anything that seriously wrong with him," he said.

"Well, you don't know what they gave him at that laboratory," she said. "What do we do?" asked Dino.

"I think we really need to leave him here on the side of the road, he will just slow us down," said Jezebel.

"Well, that's pretty cold if you ask me," said Dino. Dino got out of the car and proceeded to pull his body out, propping him up against the tree.

"Ahh Jez, I feel really awful doing this, I feel so bad for him."

"Dino, he is dead, he didn't have a chance from the beginning when this doctor got hold of him. We need to get out of here," said Jez.

"Where should we go?" asked Dino.

"We can't go back to my house, and certainly not yours."

"I think the police thought that I killed your roommate, so I have to be very careful, I've been at too many crime scenes lately," said Dino.

"Yes," she said, "you're right, when I was looking for you earlier, I went to your office and it was crawling with cops. Then I thought you just might be at Humberto's."

"How did you know about Humberto's?" he asked. "I never mentioned it before to you."

"Oh, sugarplum, I have a way of finding out information when I need it. I think we ought to stay at the Shady Dog Motel, it's right up the road here," she said.

He gave her a look of uncertainty. "Yeah, I guess so," he said.

CHAPTER SEVEN

They pulled into the Shady Dog Motel and went into the office to check in. He walked her to her room. Looking into Dino's eyes, she slid her arms around his neck and said, "Goodnight, sugar," and gave him a long passionate kiss.

"Oh! Doll face, you are really somethin'." He felt it hard to ignore the thumping of his heart and the tickling from the pit of his stomach.

She turned and went into her room and him to his. He lay down on the bed, very awestruck. "What a dame," he said.

He fell asleep and dreamed of Jezebel running on the beach, with her hair flowing in the wind, long legs gracefully taking strides like a gazelle leaping through the forest, her ears blowing straight back, her movement so fluid. There was a man moving quickly upon her as he threw a noose around her neck, pulling her backwards. She was screaming and struggling, trying to pull free from the noose as he roped her in and stuck her in a cage that was sitting on the beach. Dino looked at the face of the man, and it was Jim Barnes.

He woke up suddenly in a cold sweat. He looked at the clock and it was 5:30 AM. He got dressed and decided to get some coffee. He opened the front door to the sun just beginning to rise. As he walked over to the local coffee shop, he went past Jezebel's car and noticed the passenger door was slightly ajar. He opened the door and saw a bloodstained note on the passenger seat. The note read, "YOU WERE WARNED!"

The fear in him was overwhelming. His first thought was Jezebel. He ran to her room and knocked on the door. No one answered. He ran to the manager's office.

"Come quickly, I need my friend's room opened up."

The manager was a short obese man and couldn't walk very fast, but he did his best in following Dino to the room. He unlocked Jezebel's room.

"Jez, are you here?" He had that same feeling all over again, the one that he had when he first walked into Jez's house and found the roommate dead. He looked in the closets and checked the carpet for any clue.

He noticed the closed bathroom door. He knocked, "Jez, are you in there?" He turned the door handle, opened the door and no one was there. A shimmer caught the corner of his eye. As he turned, he saw the sunlight peering in through the window against a gemstone that was lying on the sink. It reflected off the stainless steel sink. There on the carpet were two stones.

He picked them up and remembered the necklace that she had never taken off. Some stones had fallen out, and he questioned if there was a struggle. He put the stones in his pocket. "Did you see anyone leave this room or anyone coming or going during the middle of the night?" Dino asked.

"Well," said the manager, "I have been here since four AM and really didn't notice any cars coming or going. However, come to think about it, there was a black Caddy that came about 4:30 this morning. I thought it was a little strange coming into the parking lot at that hour of the morning, but I didn't give it too much thought. Besides, I can't see everything that goes on in every room. You know, though, I didn't see the car leave."

Dino said, "Let's go to the parking lot."

They looked around and saw a black Cadillac parked about seven rooms down from Dino's room. "Is that the car you saw?" asked Dino.

"Yeah, I believe so," said the manager.

They walked over to the car and looked through the windows.

Dino noticed a piece of clothing hanging from the trunk. He opened the trunk very slowly, and there lay the limp body of Lackahair.

Dino cried out, "Oh, no!"

He picked her up and held her in his arms for a moment, feeling as though someone had just ripped his heart out. He looked down at her clenched fist. In her hand was a note that read, "Midnight on Pier 12." He took the note and put it in his pocket.

The manager just stood there, watching him and said, "What is going on here, sir? I think we should call the police." Dino kept on staring at her.

"Sir, sir, please answer me. I can't leave this car here like this with her in it."

"Yes, yes, I hear you," replied Dino. Dino laid her back down, took out a handkerchief and began wiping down the door handles and the trunk to get rid of any fingerprints, knowing that he once again might be a suspect.

"I don't think you should be doing that, sir," said the manager.

"Look, you don't know the whole story. I had nothing to do with this, but I know I'll be blamed for this just by being here."

"I don't think so. You just need to explain to the police," said the manager.

"No, they will never believe this one. It is a very long story, and I need to get out of here. I need to find my friend who was in the next room. Time is running out," said Dino.

Dino went back into Jezebel's room to look for any other clues that might still be there. There was not a trace of her.

He got into the Jaguar, searching for an extra key that might be hidden somewhere. He looked in the glove compartment and under the dash. Under the right front fender was a little magnetic box with the key inside. He got back into the car and drove out to the highway, heading toward the city.

CHAPTER EIGHT

He drove aimlessly. He was so distraught that he didn't know what to do.

After several hours, he decided to go back to the doctor's house. So he headed out to the road where Jezebel had taken him last night. He drove up the road and parked behind some bushes that faced the house.

It was early in the afternoon. He sat in the car for about one hour just watching, when a black and white police car pulled up in front, and there were the two cops who cornered him and Lackahair.

He watched them walk up to the house and knock on the big, beautiful steel doors. The door opened and a tall man came out, yelling at the police officers. Dino couldn't understand what he was yelling about, but he was pointing at their car as if to tell them to leave. It was very difficult to make out who the man was, but Dino guessed that it must have been the doctor.

Dino continued to wait. He began to look through the glove compartment of Jezebel's car, where he found pictures of Jezebel with her boss, Mr. Tyson, and strangely enough, a man who looked like Barnes but with blond hair. He thought to himself, very odd that Barnes was in the picture, he didn't realize that Jez even knew Jim Barnes that well except for the connection after the disappearance of Mrs. Barnes. Jezebel was dressed in a black evening gown, and the two men were in tuxedos. He also found a book of matches from a place called the "The Cocky Dog."

Dino thought to himself, something stinks here. He opened the note that he found in Lackahair's hand and wondered, "What night at midnight, and what was going to take place? What was she trying to tell him?"

Dino's gaze went up to the second story window, and there was a silhouette of a woman standing there, with long hair, and a long sleek nose.

"Jezebel," he thought. "Did the doctor kidnap her? Could that be her in the window? I need to find out if that is her and get her out of there." She then disappeared from the window. He wanted to go after her now. Nevertheless, he needed more evidence if he were going to go in alone.

He lit a cigar and continued to sit and think for a while longer. He decided to head on over to the racetrack. He knew the police were looking for him, so he wanted to disguise himself. He remembered seeing a hat shop back in the city.

He drove until he came to a place called Harry's Hat Shop on Lexington Avenue. He pulled up in front of the shop, where he saw Harry's face plastered all over the front window. Inside the shop was the owner, Harry, a tall Scottish deerhound wearing a green and red kilt and with long, hairy, skinny legs. His green felt hat had a long feather sticking up.

The deerhound walked over to him and asked something that Dino couldn't quite understand. Harry's Scottish accent was so heavy; Dino couldn't understand what he was saying. He asked again, "Lad, do you need some help?"

"Are you talkin' to me?" Dino asked. "First, my name isn't lad, and yes, I'm lookin' for a hat."

"Well, you sure came to the right place. We have round hats, tall hats, square hats, wide hats, caps of any color," said Harry.

"Okay, okay. I just need a plain old cap," said Dino.

"Sure, lad," as he pulled out his ladder and climbed to the top shelf. Dino took out a cigar and lit it while Harry was searching for a hat. Harry began to cough from the top of the ladder.

"What is that smell in my shop? No, you don't want to be doin' that, you need to take that thing outside," Harry said.

Dino walked out the front door and put his cigar out on the sidewalk, came back in, and Harry had found a black cap with a bill on it and gave it to him.

"Hey, aren't you the lad in the paper?"

"What paper? I don't know what you are talking about." "You know, you know, that private eye guy."

"No, no, that is not me. You have me mistaken for somebody else." "Ahh, you're a colorful lad," said Harry.

Dino put the cap on and walked over to the mirror, thinking how cool he looked. "I'll take it."

"That will be $26.95."

He drove into the back of the racetrack parking lot in case someone recognized Jezebel's car.

He walked through the revolving doors that led into the track and again saw all the same greyhound cashiers. He walked over to where the executive offices were and very inconspicuously tried the locked main door. He stood and waited for a while, and then the door opened and a man walked out. He went up the stairs to Tyson's office. He walked over to the receptionist, a short woman with glasses.

He knew he could charm this one. He looked at her and smiled, "Hi, beautiful. I am with the police department, and I need to get into Mr. Tyson's office to examine a few things."

"Well, I don't know, sir; it's all locked up now. I thought the police were all through in there," she said.

"Well, we are, but I believe there is something that we overlooked."

Dino gazed into her eyes, saying, "Did anyone ever tell you that you have the most beautiful baby blues, wow, those eyes are gorgeous. I'll bet you have all the men just flocking around you."

"Why, no, sir," she said as her face turned beet red. "You are embarrassing me," as she giggled. She, smitten by his charm, handed him the key to the office and said, "Why don't you come back and see me on the way out?"

"Thanks, gorgeous," he said.

He went in and closed the door behind him. Dino noticed the papers scattered all over the desk as though nothing had been touched.

The drops of blood were still on the carpet. He began opening up the drawers and noticed the same funny-looking matchbook cover with a dog on it with a very long tail and a red bandana around his head that read, "The Cocky Dog." He asked himself, "Did they both frequent the same place?"

He continued looking through the drawers and found pictures of all the greyhound cashiers and pictures of Tyson and Mrs. Barnes. As he continued to look, he reached to the back of the drawer and pulled out a magazine titled *The Clone Age*. He thumbed through it, and it appeared to be a medical book.

What was the connection between Tyson and the doctor?

The door flew open and five police officers came barreling in, yelling, "Put your hands up, Vicelli! You are under arrest for the murder of Lackahair Thomas and for the kidnapping of Jezebel Collins."

"What? What is this all about? I never killed or kidnapped anyone. Don't you know who I am?" he asked.

They took him out past the little receptionist who let him in, as she and everyone else just watched. Then they shoved him into the police car.

"How did you do it, Vicelli?"

"Do what? Look, I know where Jezebel Collins is. I can take you to her.

As for Lackahair, I don't know who killed her." "And just where is Miss Collins?"

"Okay, I am pretty sure she is at the house of a doctor by the name of Senrab."

"Are you serious, do you know that he is one of the most prominent, influential men in this town?

"Well, I am telling you, I think I saw her through a window."

"You will say anything to get your neck out of the noose," they both chuckled.

"Wait a minute; I have the doctor's shoes in the back of the Jaguar parked in the lot to have tested. There is blood on them."

"How did you get them?" "I broke into his house."

"Oh, so now we got you for breaking and entering as well."

"Come on, Vicelli, you have been at every crime scene. If you are not guilty, I would find that very hard to believe."

They walked him into the police station where there sat the desk sergeant, who was a large Great Dane. "Hey, Vicelli, what are you here for?"

"They are trying to pin a murder rap on me," said Dino.

"Hey boys, this is Dino Vicelli, he ain't never done nothin' to no one.

He's as clean as they come."

"Well, we were told to bring him in, and according to several eyewitnesses and prints, he looks pretty guilty."

"Really, I find that hard to believe. I will dig into it further for you, Vicelli. Do you have a good lawyer?"

They threw Dino into a cell with a very wiry-looking, scruffy Airedale Terrier. Dino sat down on the bench, when the Airedale came strolling up to him, cigarette in his mouth. "Hey man, you got a light?"

Dino looked at him with disgust. "No, I don't," he said. "What are you in here for, man?" asked the Airedale. "Look, pal, I'm not much on conversation today."

"Okay? Okay, sorry, sorry, so touchy. Well they accused me of trying to rob a hot dog stand, now can you believe that?"

Dino could hear his voice but wasn't paying a bit of attention, as he was lost in his own thoughts and problems. Dino sat and waited for hours, as he thought to himself, how long would this idiot ramble on?

Dino now had the time to sit and reflect on what had actually transpired in the last week. The more he thought, the more depressed he became. He remembered when he was a small boy growing up and his father, who was also a private investigator, told him, "never to fall hard for a dame. Boy, was he right," thought Dino.

Finally, he saw an officer walking toward his cell with keys in his hand. "Hey, Vicelli, too bad that you couldn't visit with us a little longer. Somebody made your bail."

"Who was that?" asked Dino. The officer didn't answer. Dino got his things and walked out the station doors.

He began walking down the cold, dimly lit New York streets, past the garbage cans. He was glad he had his tan overcoat with him to keep his body protected from the bitter cold chill in the air. The wind was blowing so hard, it left a sting on his skin.

As he continued to walk, he began to hear another set of footsteps walking behind him. He paused and turned around and no one was there. He continued to walk, thinking that maybe it was his imagination. Again, the sounds of footsteps haunted him. He yelled out, "Who's there? You don't want to mess with me, whoever you are." He looked all around and still couldn't see anyone. Then he felt a tap on his shoulder.

He turned around and said, "Barnes?" "Yes, it's me," said Barnes.

"What are you doin' here?" asked Dino.

"Well, I would think that you would be a little friendlier toward me since I made your bail," said Barnes.

"You, you made my bail?"

"Yes, Vicelli, it was me. It's really gone too far. I felt bad for you taking the rap for everything that has been going on. If you had gotten off this case earlier, it wouldn't have gone this far."

"Do you know who killed Lackahair and what happened to Jezebel?" asked Dino.

"I really don't know who those people are that you are talking about?" "Yes you do, Barnes; she is your wife's predecessor."

"Oh, you are talking about the tall pretty blonde at Tyson's office." "Yeah, well, she is missing now."

"Vicelli, how would I know that?" "Why did you really make bail for me?"

"Boy, talk about looking a gift horse in the mouth. I told you that I felt guilty dragging you into this and then throwing you to the dogs, so to speak."

"That wasn't your attitude the other day."

"No, well, I have had some time to think, Vicelli. I have just been so upset about my wife. I have to go, but watch your back."

CHAPTER NINE

He took the subway and got off about a block away from his office. As he walked down the street, he passed the newspaper stand, and out of the corner of his eye, he saw a familiar face on the front page of the newspaper that looked like him. It took a minute to register as he kept walking, then he turned around quickly and did a double take. He could not believe his eyes, saying, "It's me."

"Sure is," said Dave, an old-time newspaper vendor who had been in that same location for the last 30 years. "You really did it this time, Vicelli. Made a big name for yourself, ha? I read the story on you, interesting." Dave handed Dino the newspaper. "This one's on me, pal. Go ahead and take it." The headline read, "*WELL-KNOWN PRIVATE EYE ARRESTED FOR MURDER.*"

He took the paper and walked to his office building, anxious to read the story. As he walked into the building, the guard said, "Mr. Vicelli, good morning, so glad to see you're out of jail."

Dino, eyeing him with disdain, walked quickly past him and into the elevator while ignoring his comment.

As he got off the elevator, he heard the two men chuckling in the office down the hall from his.

"Did you see this picture of that old hound dog?"

"Yeah, real well-known detective. He's a bumbling idiot, and I sure wouldn't want him on any case of mine," as they laughed.

Dino tiptoed past their office; he didn't need to make any waves with these jokers. He just didn't need any more trouble. He went into his office and closed the door, walking into the same mess that he had left.

He sat down in his chair, stretched his feet up onto the desk and lit a cigar, using the book of matches that he found in Tyson's office. He sat there and thought of poor Lackahair and how her life ended so quickly. He never had a chance with her.

He knew he had to clear his name, but didn't know just how he would do it. Dino opened the paper and continued to read about a private investigator arrested for killing an FBI agent who worked undercover at Humberto's Bar and Grill. "What?" said Dino loudly.

He thought to himself that it was funny how he never knew that she was an FBI agent. He remembered watching the little dame move up and down the bar, thinking how gorgeous she was. Pangs of guilt overtook him as he thought about her.

He happened to look up at that moment and noticed a man standing at his door. The door opened.

"Mr. Vicelli, I have a delivery for you."

"Oh, okay." The boy looked to be about 19 years old, tall, had brown hair and wore glasses. The boy handed him the package. "Can you please sign here?"

Dino looked at the envelope, looked at the boy, and said, "Sure thing, kid. Who sent you?"

The boy didn't answer. He waited until the boy left and opened the package. As he opened it, the folded piece of paper inside and a lock of golden blonde hair fell onto his desk. A letter read, "Vicelli, if you want to see her again, meet me tonight at 8 P.M. at the Tail of the Dog, by yourself, no police."

Dino was so glad to hear that Jezebel was still alive. He sat there and played with her lock of hair, running the hair through his fingers, dreaming of how beautiful she was. He jumped up and ran to the door to see where the delivery boy was, but he was long gone.

He continued to look through the package and found a picture of Jezebel and a very handsome African-American man. He couldn't help but wonder who this man was. He had never seen him before. He looked at his watch and noticed it was 6 P.M.

The door opened and two suits flashed their badges in Dino's face. "Mr. Vicelli, we're with the FBI, may we have a word with you?"

"Why not, sit down, gentlemen." They stepped over the broken glass, books and papers that were on the floor.

"Mr. Vicelli, we have been following the man you know as Mr. Barnes. We believe that there may be some connection between the murder of our FBI agent, Lackahair Thomas, and him. We have been tailing him for quite some time now. We are here to find out exactly what you know about this man."

"Well, I don't know as much as I would like to," said Dino. "Jim Barnes is very mysterious, you know, just kind of hard to figure out."

"Why did he bail you out?"

"I don't quite know. This whole situation goes back to about four weeks ago, and it is a long story, gentlemen, longer than I have time for right now."

"Are you going somewhere, Mr. Vicelli?"

"Well, no, just have to take care of something personal."

"Well, we won't take up any more of your time. If you need to reach us for anything at all that you may remember, here is the number. By the way, I would be very careful if I were you. I wouldn't trust all that you see."

Dino gazed down at one of the agents' hands, where there was a very small white star drawn on the top of his hand. He didn't want the agent to know that he had noticed it.

"Can I see your badges again?"

"Mr. Vicelli, I don't think that is necessary. We will be back when you have some more time."

"Why are you trying to find out what I know about him? Are you afraid I know too much?" asked Dino.

"We don't know what you are talking about, Mr. Vicelli."

"We will let you get on your way, Mr. Vicelli." They walked out the door while Dino sat for a few minutes, waiting until he was sure that they were gone.

He picked up the phone to call his attorney, Bill Weiler.

He heard the woman's nasal-sounding voice at the other end of the phone.

"Weiler and Weiler," she said. "Yes, ahh, Mr. Weiler, please." "Who's calling?"

"Dino Vicelli."

"Would you like Bill or Rot?"

"Oh, ahh, Bill please, by the way, when did he bring his son Rot into the business?"

"Rot Weiler has been with us for about a year. Just one moment, Mr.

Vicelli, and I will put you through to Mr. Weiler."

Dino could not help but recognize that loud, jolly voice at the other end of the phone.

"Vicelli, how are you? Haven't heard from you in quite a long time." "Yeah, Bill, I am doing okay, but I seem to have got myself into a little jam here."

"What do you mean? You are always in a jam, but you have always got yourself out of it."

"Not this time, Bill, been arrested for murder. Someone made my bail, so I am out for now, but I think I am going to need your services."

"Well, why don't we plan on meeting tomorrow for coffee, and I will see what I can do to help you out."

"Okay, how about the Lucky Paws coffee shop at ten in the morning?" "See you then, Vicelli."

CHAPTER TEN

Dino's cab pulled up to the dark blue two-story glass building, where flashing neon lights read, "TAIL OF THE DOG."

"This is it," said the driver. Dino paid him and got out.

He walked into a very loud, disco-type atmosphere with bright colored lights swirling around the room. He looked down and noticed he was walking on glass block floors.

The cigarette smoke was so thick that he had a hard time seeing where he was going. He felt right at home, though.

"Beautiful joint," he thought. He walked over to the light blue, high back velvet barstools that were shaped like large dog bones and sat down.

The bartender, who was a short bearded collie, came over and said, "What can I get you, bud?"

Dino replied, "I'll have a salty dog." "Sure," said the bartender.

Dino sat and looked down the crowded bar and glanced at the cages set up along the dance floor. He had always heard about places like this. "Hmmm," he thought, "this is where they have the dancing disco dogs." He sat there for a couple of minutes, just studying people. Then the music started, and sure enough, out walked the dancers, beautiful thin long-legged salukis.

Dino watched them as they sauntered out onto the stage and into the cages. Wow, he thought, they are so beautiful, almost like Jezebel. He watched them as their hips swayed side to side, their tails flinging all around, and the graceful shifting, of their bodies, gently moving to the music. He was entranced with their grace and elegance.

They wore costumes made of silk. Short blue skirts with tied tops and long flowing sleeves.

Dino took out a cigar and started to put it into his mouth, when someone from behind lit his cigar. "Dino Vicelli?" the voice said. Dino looked down at the black leather glove that was lighting his cigar. He looked up into the face of a tall African-American man.

Dino knew right away that this was his contact, the man in the picture seen with Jezebel. The man was dressed very chic, in a black pin-striped suit. This big, tall man with his deep voice was a little intimidating to Dino.

Dino said, "Yeah, that's me."

"I thought so, I recognized you from your picture in the paper. I'm Byron Scone."

"Well, why don't you sit down, Mr. Scone?"

"Better yet, why don't we grab a table over there?" said Scone.

Dino took his drink and followed Scone over to the table. He picked a table that was far away from the dance floor and the cages, so as not to get distracted.

"Well, I guess you have really had a lot of bad publicity lately, it looks like you're in some real trouble."

"Yeah, I am, I need some answers and quick. I'm hoping you're the one who can give me those answers, Mr. Scone. What do you know about the disappearance of Jezebel Collins? Did you kidnap her?" Dino puffed on his cigar, looking very intently, waiting for Scone to speak.

"The players in this little charade, Mr. Vicelli, are a lot more dangerous than you think."

"How do you know? How do you fit into all of this?" asked Dino. "Well, your friend Mr. Barnes—"

Dino interrupted, "Wait a minute, how do you know Barnes?"

"How do I know? I will tell you. I was hired to kill his wife, but I didn't. Too many people wanted her dead. She knew too much about the operation at the track, and so did Tyson. You see, there is a lot of money being made by the good old doctor, and it's not from the betting profits. The track is just a cover for a bigger operation pertaining to cloning animals and people."

Dino, with a very puzzled look on his face, said "You're talkin' in riddles, Scone."

"Oh, yeah, and Miss Jezebel Collins is not who you think she is. Try tying her and Katy Barnes in together. I am not one hundred percent sure, but I can bet you they're one and the same…"

"WHAT," yelled Dino. The surprise in his voice was so loud that the crowds of people surrounding them heard him over the loud music and all turned around.

Dino, sitting there shocked, put his head in hands, covering his eyes and staring down at the table. "I don't believe this," said Dino.

"I was also hired to kill Jezebel, but I made a mistake and killed her roommate instead."

"That was you who killed her roommate?" "Yes," said Scone.

"Who was the redheaded man who was at her house then? I thought that he killed her," asked Dino.

"Oh, a tall redheaded fellow?" asked Scone. "Yes," said Dino.

"That was Senrab's assistant; he does a lot of Senrab's dirty work. Clean up, you know, to get rid of the body type of thing.

"You see, the doctor doesn't take too kindly to people he wants to keep for his own and then they leave him. He would have rather seen her dead than live without her."

"Does she know any of this?" asked Dino. "That is the craziest thing I've ever heard."

"You see, he has a big operation in smuggling dogs and people in from overseas. He clones and also does transformations and gets the big bucks from someone who is looking for a worker or mate, or whatever they may need, to be more robotic and just almost made to order, personality-wise, work-wise, etc. Senrab controls them by the stars on their bodies."

As Dino sat there puffing on his cigar, he said, "Come on, we all know that people have been racing on the track for years. This is the world we live in. Dogs have their fair positions in life, but this is a little farfetched. I have a hard time believing this crazy story. However, the star that you are talking about I remember seeing. It was in the doctor's front yard. A light was shining into the sky in the shape of the star."

"Tyson was the doctor's partner. I was told to kill him; he was getting a little too greedy," said Scone.

"Why are you telling me this, Scone? I could turn you in to the police right now."

"I am telling you this because I am the only one who can help you get your precious Jezebel back. Besides that, I may be the next one he decides to kill because I know too much. I am going to turn myself in to the police. I feel that is the safest thing for me to do now."

"Where is Jezebel now?" Dino asked. "I will show you where," said Scone.

Dino looked up and noticed a beautiful, tall, dark slender woman walking through the smoke-filled crowded room, headed straight toward their table.

Dino looked at Scone and started to ask him if he knew the woman was coming over. She approached the table and bent down to whisper in Scone's ear.

He began gasping for air.

"What is the matter, Scone? What is it?"

Scone's eyes were bulging out of his head. Dino got up, looked down, and saw a knife protruding from his ribs on the right side. Blood was running down his well pressed white shirt under his pinstriped suit.

Dino jumped up and yelled loudly over the music, "Someone get an ambulance!" as Scone's body slumped over the table. He watched the woman run to the front door. Dino bent down to tell Scone to "hold on for the ambulance." People were screaming in a wild panic.

Dino knew he had to get out of there before the police arrived. He quickly got up and ran past the bar, telling the bartender to call the police and make sure that an ambulance was on its way. He ran through the hazy room full of panic and made his way through the front door.

As he walked out the door, he saw all the flashing lights and heard the sirens coming down the street.

The air was cold and thick with fog. He walked about a block down, looked back, and saw Scone taken away on a stretcher. He hoped that Scone would make it.

He wandered through the fog, absorbing all that he had just heard. Dino had to pay close attention to where he was going, as the fog was so thick and the night was so dark, only lit by the very faint light from the tall street lamps. He found a bus stop and sat down, wondering what to do next. He knew he had to have a plan. He knew he had to get back into the doctor's house. He had to find Jezebel, and, "Why was Lackahair killed? Did they know she was an FBI agent? Who was Jezebel really?" There were so many unanswered questions that Scone never got the chance to explain.

He continued to sit there, trying to work out the pieces to this puzzle, as the heavy fog continued to roll in. He noticed how there was not a soul on the streets; the quietness in the air was almost eerie. He reached in his pocket, pulled out the matchbook from the club, and began just staring at it. Then he heard the sound of footsteps walking very quickly from behind him. Dino started to turn around, when he felt the jolt of something very heavy hitting the back of his neck, almost as though someone had taken a hammer and pounded it right into his neck. He felt his neck drop into his chest as he fell onto the bench.

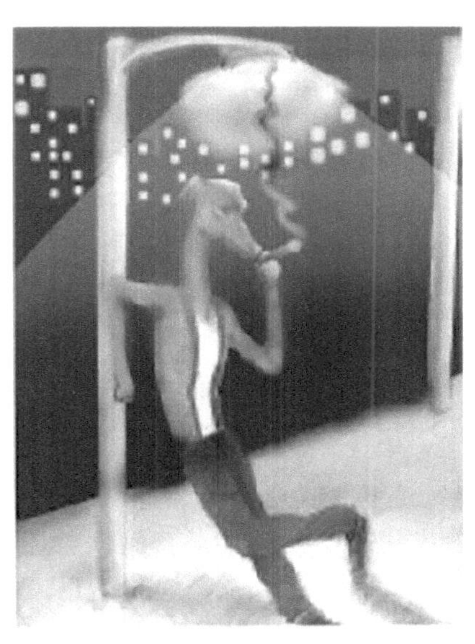

CHAPTER ELEVEN

The smell of pine was in the air as Dino began to open his eyes. He didn't understand; his eyes were open and it was pitch black. He reached to the back of his neck to feel the large sore bump as his elbow hit something. He couldn't reach very far. He felt as though he were in a box. He managed to reach into his pocket, took out the matches, and lit one to the surroundings of a coffin.

Panic began to set in as he tried to calm himself, trying not to use up all of his oxygen. He put out the match very quickly, wondering what to do now. He heard voices of men coming from the outside. "What do we do with this one?"

"I don't know, this is the new one that just came in, there is another one there from earlier tonight as well."

"Why don't we wait and see where we should put them?"

"Yeah, let's leave them for now." Dino heard the footsteps of the men walk away. He knew that he had to get out of there quickly. He began scratching and pushing at the top of the box, but nothing was happening.

He heard scratching and digging from above. Then he heard whimpering. "It's a dog," he thought. Dino lay still, hoping the dog would dig him out of there. Dino jumped up and hit his head as he felt the wet flow coming on to his face.

"Oh, you mangy mutt," he yelled. There were voices speaking in Spanish, and he couldn't quite understand what they were saying. He could hear the shovel digging while dirt fell through the cracks onto his face.

"Hey, boss, look. He is alive. We thought that he was dead." They opened the box, and Dino stood up and brushed himself off.

He looked up and said, "Barnes what are you doing here? What kind of game are you playin' with me?"

"I am not playing any game with you; you are supposed to be dead. You have caused me a lot of trouble, Mr. Vicelli. This time I will have to kill you myself."

Dino scowled at him. "I don't get it, Barnes, who are you?"

"Gentlemen, take him to the warehouse. I wouldn't mind having the little short greyhound working for us."

They went to grab Dino's arm, and Dino punched the assistant in the stomach. The other grabbed him, and Dino kicked him in the leg. Both men grabbed him and pinned him against the wall. They tied his hands from behind and blindfolded him.

The car trip was long, and he didn't know where they were taking him. They finally stopped, and he heard the sound of a rolling door opening. He thought that maybe it was a storage area.

They pulled him from the car, took him inside and took the blindfold off. Dino saw that it was a large warehouse with lots of pine boxes lying on the floor. The man he thought to be Barnes was not with them. It was only the two assistants.

They tied him to a pole.

"You stay here for a while, Vicelli. We have to leave, but we will be back."

"Hey, you can't just leave me here tied to a pole," yelled Dino.

They walked out and closed the warehouse door. Dino, standing there helpless, didn't quite know how to get out of this one. He stood for what seemed for hours, as he finally started to get tired of standing and sunk to the ground. Groaning sounds were coming from one of the boxes.

"Someone help me," the soft voice said. "Who is there?" said Dino.

"Dino, is that you, it's me, Jezebel." "Jezebel, are you all right?" asked Dino.

"Dino, I am so weak, I need your help, please."

"I am going to try to work my way loose from these ropes, hang in there, Jez."

Dino kept working his hands back and forth, trying to work his way out of them. Finally, the ropes began to loosen.

He got loose and ran to the boxes. "Jezebel, talk to me, I need to know which one you are in."

"Over here, Dino."

He ran over to the box that she was in and began to pry it open with a tire iron that had been sitting there. He bent down and lifted her up out of the box.

"Jezebel, what happened? What are you doing here?"

"Oh, Dino, it was so awful. He wants me for himself and I refused him, so he told his assistants to kill me. They put me in this awful box." The tears rolled down her eyes as her deep sobs left her breathless.

"Oh, Jez, I am so sorry. We have to get out of here now, before they come back."

"Dino, I saw something on one of those boxes, before they put me in here. I have to know."

"What, Jez?" asked Dino.

"Do you remember I told you that I had a friend who was missing? I saw his name on one of those boxes. I have to find out if it is him."

"Okay, which one?"

"The first one over there," she said.

Dino pried open the first box, and as he opened it, Jezebel let out a loud gasp.

"It's him, it's Gerard." "How do you know?"

"I know by the ring on his finger, I gave it to him," she said. She pulled the ring off his finger and put it down into her bra. "We might need it for evidence, and not only that, he was my friend and I want it for memory."

"What are you doing?" asked Dino.

"It has a lot of sentimental value, Dino." "Okay, let's please get out of here."

The loud squealing of brakes came rolling up to the warehouse.

"They are back, I told you we had to get out of here!" He grabbed her arm. He pulled her over to a big steel drum as they climbed in.

The large roller door opened. "Where did he go? Vicelli is gone."

Dino started to say something, and Jezebel put her finger to her mouth to say "SHHH."

"Check the grounds inside and out. Look, she is gone as well. He got loose and let her out."

They heard the doctor rambling on, "You stupid idiots, why didn't one of you stay with him and one of you come and get me? What do I pay you for?"

While huddled together very quietly, they heard footsteps all around them. Jezebel was breathing very loudly, and Dino motioned for her to be quiet.

"Boss, I don't think they are in here, there is really nowhere they could be hiding. I think they may have gone outside."

"Well, find them and quick," said Senrab.

Senrab turned around and faced the steel drum that Jez and Dino were in and said, "Shhh." They walked over to the drum. Dino listened to every footstep coming toward them. Jezebel's breathing became heavier and heavier. Dino felt his heart pounding through his chest.

He whispered to her, "When I say go, I want to rock this thing over on its side.

You take my hand, and we are going to run as fast as we can. Do you understand?"

"Yes," she nodded.

The footsteps stopped as though they had paused for a moment.

"Go," Dino said. As they knocked the drum over, it began to roll. They rolled and rolled until the drum ran into a wall. The doctor and his assistants were running after the drum. Dino grabbed her hand, and they began to run out the door. One of the assistants shot at them but missed. They ran into a wooded area and kept running until they came to a ravine, which they crossed. They finally rested behind a tree.

"I think we lost them," said Dino.

"Look, Dino there is a fence up there with the highway on the other side."

They ran to the fence and climbed over it, hoping they could get a ride into town. They walked along the road for miles, and then they saw headlights coming their way. Dino waved his arms and flagged down a car. As Dino looked at the man, he noticed it was one of the doctor's assistants.

"Hey, Mr. Vicelli, how ya doin'? Everyone is looking for you."

The man pulled out a gun and said, "Get in." Jezebel climbed into the back seat and Dino in the front, all the while staring at a gun barrel.

"I guess you're both ready to go back now." The man began to drive. Dino quickly grabbed the man's arm, knocking the revolver onto the seat. Dino began to fight with him, causing the man to lose control of the car, and the struggle became intense. The car weaved back and forth, the driver trying to regain control but unable, finally losing control and running the car right into a tree. Jezebel's head went flying right into the headrest of the front seat, and Dino's head went right into the front windshield. The driver was thrown onto the hood of the car.

Dino and Jezebel lay there in the car all night until the sun began to rise. Jezebel opened her eyes to the bright ray of sunshine peeking through the branches of trees that lay over the car.

"Uhmmm," she moaned, "Dino? Dino? Are you there? Are you all right?"

She put her hands to her forehead, feeling the dried blood on her fur. She reached forward and pulled Dino away from the windshield. "Dino, wake up," she said.

She climbed out of the driver's side of the car and went around to the front passenger side where Dino lay unconscious.

"Dino, I have to get you to a hospital." She went to the hood of the car and dragged the driver's body off the car and into the bushes. Panic set in as she began to cry.

She got in and turned the key, but the car wouldn't start. She kept trying, turning the key and stepping on the accelerator, until finally the car started. She backed out of the tree and drove up onto the road. The car was barely running, but she kept driving.

As they kept driving, she noticed a set of headlights coming up close behind her. She looked over at Dino and he was out cold. She knew it was the doctor chasing them down. Then there were flashing lights as a police car drove right past her and in front of her, motioning to slow down and pull over.

She then pulled over and was so relieved to see a police officer, while the cars behind her kept going straight as she watched them drive off. A tall dark-haired police officer came walking up to her window and said, "Ma'am is everything all right? Were you part of the accident back there?"

Jezebel was unable to speak. He then bent down and looked to the passenger seat at Dino.

He walked around and opened the door, lifting Dino's paw to feel his pulse.

"He needs to get to a hospital right away," he said.

Jezebel broke down and began to sob. "What do we do? We need your help, officer," said Jezebel.

"I will call to give you an escort into the city, ma'am," said the officer. "I think that would be quicker than trying to get an ambulance all the way out here. I checked the man back there and he appears to be dead. Just follow me," he said.

Jezebel followed the flashing red lights as the sirens screeched loudly. They got into the city and drove up to the curb in front of the hospital. The paramedics greeted them while putting Dino onto a stretcher and taking him in.

She held Dino's hand as they put him on the stretcher and wheeled him into the examination room.

Jezebel waited in the waiting room for what seemed like eternity. The doctor came out one hour later and said, "He is fine, just some nasty cuts and bruises. We x-rayed his head and found no internal bleeding. He needed stitches in his head, and he will be able to leave in a couple of hours. He is still unconscious now, but give him a little time." Jezebel was so relieved that he was okay.

Meanwhile, back at the doctor's house, rage was on the rampage. "Where is she?" he screamed to his assistants. He was so enraged that she was gone.

He was smashing expensive vases and different glass items.

"I want her found immediately. I pay you to guard," as he threw a vase right past one of the Dobermans' heads.

"How did you miss Vicelli, no doubt they are probably both together? How did they get out of there? I would like to know." The guards and the assistants just stood there in silence, listening to his ranting and raving.

Jezebel continued to wait for Dino. Then she saw him walking down the hall very slowly toward her. She ran up to him and grabbed his arm to help him. "I'm going to take good care of you," she said. Dino was very quiet, feeling a little tired.

CHAPTER TWELVE

They walked out of the hospital, passing the assistant's car. Jezebel grabbed a cab, and they went back to Dino's place. They walked in and Dino fell on the bed in a deep sleep.

Jezebel sat and watched Dino sleep, then finally lay down on the bed next to him, drifting off into a deep slumber while listening to the quiet snoring next to her.

Hours later, the loud ring of the telephone awakened her. She answered, "Hello."

"Why did you run off so quickly, my dear? You know I will get you back, don't you? I will find you and hunt you down, and you will never leave me again."

She slammed down the phone. Shaking Dino, she said, "Wake up, wake up." Dino rolled over to see the tears running down Jezebel's face.

"What's the matter, Jez? Why are you so upset?"

"Dino, we will never be at peace until that man is either in jail or dead." "Who?" asked Dino.

"That was Dr. Senrab on the phone. He said he is going to find me and kill me. I'm really scared now," said Jezebel.

"How did he get my phone number? Well, we have to get out of here. Don't worry, Jez, I wont let him hurt you," as he wiped the tears from her face. "We'll find a nice little motel for a while, I don't think it's safe to come back here for quite some time. I will lock everything up."

Dino grabbed a small suitcase out of his closet and grabbed some clothes. He went to the back door to lock it, when he noticed a shadow of a man standing to the right of the back door. He tiptoed over to the door and slowly turned the doorknob. The door flew open into his face, knocking him against the cabinet. Then he saw a badge flash before his face.

"Vicelli, we're putting you under arrest for the murder of Mr. Byron Scone."

Just then Dr. Senrab walked over to Vicelli as they were handcuffing him.

"I want him arrested for breaking and entering as well. You broke into my house, Mr. Vicelli."

Jezebel came running into the room. "Why, what is ever goin' on here?

Ahh, what are you doing here?" as she looked into the face of Dr. Senrab. "You can't take him, you are handcuffing the wrong person. You should be arresting that one. He is a murderer."

Dino felt the handcuffs binding so tightly around his wrists. "Do you think you can loosen these a little bit?" They pushed him out of the house and into the squad car.

Dr. Senrab walked over to Jezebel, grabbing her by the arm. "Did you really think that you could ever be free of me?"

Jezebel pulled her arm away, running out the door, yelling, "Officer!" "No need for that, Jezebel, I am leaving now, but I will see you very soon."

Dr Senrab walked out the door abruptly.

"Jezebel," Dino yelled. "I have an attorney. Call him for me. His number is in the red book under Bill Weiler." She stood and watched them drive away.

She ran back into the house and straight to the phone, looking through the red book that was lying on the desk. She looked under W for Weiler. She found it and quickly dialed the number.

She heard the woman say, "Weiler and Weiler, may I help you?" Jezebel was frantic, speaking so quickly and not very clearly that the woman asked her to slow down.

"The police arrested my friend and he asked me to call Mr. Weiler for help."

"Okay," the woman said. "Would you like senior or junior?" "I don't know," said Jezebel.

"Well, what is your friend's name?" asked the woman." "Dino Vicelli," said Jezebel.

"Ahhh," said the woman, "that would be Mr. Weiler, senior, and he is not in right now. I expect him in any minute. Would you like to leave a number?"

"Please tell him it is urgent. The police just took him to jail."

Jezebel hung up the phone, not knowing what to do. She called a taxi to take her down to the precinct. She sat down on the couch, waiting.

She noticed a photo album lying on the coffee table. As she began to thumb through it, there were pictures of when Dino was a young dog, standing with a dog in police uniform. At the bottom of the picture, it said, "Dad and Dino." Then there was a picture of a tall blonde afghan standing with Dino and his dad. It said, "Mom, Dino and Dad" and the year.

She couldn't help but note to herself the similarity between herself and his mother. It was strange that Dino never mentioned too much about his family. In the back of the album were newspaper clippings. She began to look through them. Some were on his mother, about her being a successful police psychologist and her dealings with some of the most criminal masterminds. The other clipping was a picture of his father receiving an award for capturing one of the most criminally insane doctors of all time.

The last article read, *"VICELLIS SHOT TO DEATH IN THEIR HOME, LEAVING A SMALL BOY HIDING FRANTICALLY IN THE CLOSET."*

Tears rolled from her eyes as she read this. "I never knew, poor Dino." She heard a horn blowing, and it was the taxi. She ran out the door,

locking it as she was leaving. As she jumped into the cab, the driver asked, "Where to, lady?"

"The fifty-first precinct," she said.

Dino was tucked away in his cell. Only this time he was there by himself, knowing he might be there for a while.

The cab dropped Jezebel off in front of the police department. She walked through the double doors and felt every eye upon her.

The whistles were so loud, and the men yelled and raved as they watched her make her way up to the desk sergeant.

"Men, men," the desk sergeant yelled, "keep it down; let's give the lady a little respect."

"Why, thank you, Mr. Sergeant, you're ever so kind."

She walked over to the sergeant, asking, "Do you know where I can find a Mr. Vicelli?" The sergeant looked down through his paperwork. "Vicelli, ha? I know him personally, a good guy if you ask me."

"Then why is he here, sir?" she asked.

"Ma'am, I am not the detective on that case, they must know something that I don't. Anyway, if you go through the door on the left where the guard is standing, someone inside that door will take you to him."

Jezebel walked past the detectives. She had very high heels on, showing off her long legs and a short red skirt. She walked through the door where a detective was standing on the other side. He took her down the long hallway while prisoners' arms were hanging out of their cells, trying to touch her as she walked by. They whistled and made the same crude comments.

She approached the cell where Dino sat on his cot. He looked so forlorn as she approached him. She grabbed on to the bars while sticking her head through, asking, "Are you okay?"

"Jezebel, I'm so glad to see you. Did you call my attorney?" "Yes, I did, sugar."

"I don't know what they think they have on me, but I have never killed anyone. They just threw me in here. I never even got a phone call."

Just then, they heard the door open and close and then loud footsteps coming down the hall. A voice yelled out, "Hey, Vicelli, you in here?"

"Yeah, Bill, I'm down here, keep walking," he yelled out to him. "It's my attorney, he made it," Dino said to Jezebel.

She turned and saw a large Rottweiler walking down the hall, wearing a black suit and a yellow tie and carrying a tan briefcase. Oh my, she thought to herself, he is huge. He looked to weigh about 250 pounds and stood at about 5'5". She could hear that he had difficult time breathing because he was so heavy as he waddled down the hall.

He walked over to the cell. "Vicelli," he said in his deep, raspy voice. "How are you, pal? Haven't seen you in a coon's age."

Dino stuck out his hand to shake.

"Bill Weiler, I want you to meet a very good friend of mine, Miss Jezebel Collins."

He eyed Jezebel. "The pleasure is all mine, Miss Collins," he said as he threw his little "hmm, hmm," laugh in.

"You can call me Jezebel," she said as she gave him a subtle disgusted look.

"You were the one who called my office," he said. "Yes," she said.

"There are two of us," he said. "I made my son, Rot, a partner in the firm. What is going on here, Vicelli?"

"I have been arrested twice here for different things. I have to get out of here, I can't keep going through this, Bill."

"I know, Vicelli, I know. I am going to make bail for you. Don't worry about a thing. I am going to go take care of it right now, just give me a couple of hours."

Jez watched him walk away. "How long has he been your attorney, Dino?" she asked.

"Oh, Bill, I have known him for about 15 years, we go way back. I always used him on cases that I worked on when I needed a little law work."

"He seems like a very strange man to me," she said.

"No, he's really not once you get to know him. He knew my parents; he goes way back with my father."

She looked at him, very puzzled. "Why don't you ever talk about your parents? I don't think I have ever heard you mention them before."

"No, I don't. It is very painful for me, so I normally don't talk about it. I will tell you someday when I feel comfortable enough with you."

"Okay, sugar, whatever you say."

"Dino, you will have to pardon me for a moment, I am going find the little girls' room. I will be right back, darling." She walked back down the hall toward the guard standing at the door. "Excuse me," she said, "where can I find the ladies' room?"

"Oh, sure," he said, "right past the main doors that you first came in."

She walked past all the detectives again, feeling a little nervous. One detective caught her eye, standing in the corner. She knew he looked familiar, but from where did she know him? She thought hard. It began to bother her that she didn't know. She went into the ladies' room and stood at the mirror thinking, and then it came to her. "Ahhh," she said. "I saw him at Dr. Senrab's house. That's it, I know it," she said, quietly talking to herself. She walked back out and passed the man again. He looked her right in the eye with a very cold hard stare, almost as though he were trying to penetrate right through her eyes. She shifted her eyes back to the door very quickly as he just sat there staring at her, sitting on the corner of his desk. She was nervous and shaking as she went over to the cell.

"What's wrong, Jez?" Dino asked.

"There is something weird going on here, Dino. I don't know what it is.

But I just saw one of Senrab's men. He is a detective here." "What?" asked Dino. "You must be mistaken."

"No, I wonder if Senrab got to him and maybe he is a plant here. We have to let your attorney know when he gets back."

Jezebel stuck her long nose through the bars and gave Dino a kiss. She turned and walked away as he went and sat on the cot in his cell.

He lay down and fell asleep. Someone whispering, "Vicelli," awakened him in the middle of the night. "Hey, Vicelli, wake up."

He woke up saying, "Who's there? Who is it?" "Shhh. The desk sergeant sent me here." "Hmmm?" said Dino. "What do you mean?" "Yeah, he wants to talk to you."

"Okay," said Dino. The guard went over and unlocked the cell. He took Dino down the hallway, through the door and over to the desk where the large Great Dane sat reading his newspaper. Dino looked around and the place was empty, maybe because it was about three o'clock in the morning.

"Vicelli, good to see you," said the Great Dane. His name happened to be Harvey Wimple. "I figured this would give you a little chance to stretch your legs." Harvey leaned over the very high desk, looking down at Dino, saying, "Ya know, Vicelli, I'm on your side. There is something funny going on here at this station, particularly with one of my men and maybe a couple of others. I need to find out what is going on around here. The phone calls that come in are very peculiar. I think you can help me find out just what is going on in this department."

Just then the door opened and a police officer walked in. "Well, we had better continue this little conversation later," said Harvey.

Dino went back to his cell.

CHAPTER THIRTEEN

The next morning, Dino heard the main door open and heavy breathing along with loud footsteps coming down the hallway.

"Vicelli, you're out of here. I got you out on bail." The guard unlocked his cell, and he was so relieved.

"Thanks, Bill, its good to be out," said Dino. "Listen, Bill, the desk sergeant seems to think something strange is going on here. He pulled me from my cell last night to tell me that, but we were interrupted and we didn't get a chance to finish talking. I think there is a conspiracy in this station."

"Oh, come on," said Bill.

"No, seriously, I think there might be," said Dino.

As they walked past the front desk, there was a man standing there talking to the detectives. Dino turned to Weiler. "That is Jim Barnes, the man who hired me."

"No, it's not, that is Judge Meyers," said Weiler.

"I know what my client looks like, and that is Jim Barnes."

"Ol' buddy, I think you've been in that cell too long," said Weiler.

Dino stood in amazement as Weiler grabbed him by the arm, leading him out the front doors.

"Come on, why don't we talk about it over dinner, there is a nice restaurant down the street that all the people from the courthouse go to. I called your girlfriend at your house and told her to meet us there."

They left the courthouse and walked about two blocks down to a restaurant called Contempt of Court. It was a place where all the local professionals went, from the judges, to attorneys down to all the clerks. It was famous for its great Italian food and service.

They walked into a dimly lit entryway and waited for the hostess to seat them.

The tall, beautiful redhead was busy taking a name from the men in front of them.

"Mr. Weiler, I will be right with you, sir." She seated the three men and came back for them. She took them to a booth, and everyone seemed to know Bill, nodding and saying "hi" as he walked by.

As they sat down, Jezebel came through the door. Behind her came the man from the police station, the judge who looked like Jim Barnes. He walked to another booth, where a heavy balding man was sitting. The man stood up and shook his hand. Dino was watching very intently. Jezebel caught his attention by saying, "Didn't you even notice that I am here?" He couldn't quite place where he had seen the heavyset man before.

"Oh, sorry Jez," said Dino. "Bill, who is that man sitting there with the judge?"

Bill turned around and said, "That is Congressman Shepherd, Herman Shepherd. If you remember, his picture was in the newspapers daily. It was a case of mistaken identity. They thought he had murdered his wife because she had been missing, and they found evidence of foul play in his home like a bloodstained knife on the floor in his kitchen. Don't you remember seeing it in the paper?" Weiler asked.

"Yeah," said Dino, "now that you mention it, I guess I do."

"Well, anyway, after they arrested him, she comes waltzing into the police station, alive and well. Frankly, I don't think they had enough to hold him anyway. Nobody ever did know where she was and what happened to her. It didn't seem to hurt his career any at all."

Jezebel looked over towards the judge's table. "Oh, my gosh, Dino, there is Doctor Senrab."

"I have already been through this with Vicelli. This man is a judge, not a doctor," said Weiler.

"The resemblance is uncanny," she said.

Just then the voices from the judge's table became louder and louder. People began to stare. Then they quieted down as they noticed that they were becoming a spectacle.

"Wow!" said Dino. "Wonder what that was all about."

Once again, their voices raised. The argument began to really heat up this time.

"No," Shepherd said, "you can't do that, she cannot go through that again, and I am not going to stand back and let you go through with your sinister plan." Then the whole table overturned, with drinks, dishes, and food crashing to the floor.

The hostess happened to be standing right near the judges' table. The judge got up and grabbed the beautiful redheaded hostess and put a knife to her throat.

"Do you want me to kill her?" he asked, looking defiantly at Shepherd. "Now, hold on," said Shepherd. "Judge, lets' talk, there is no need to resort to this."

Silence fell over the room as people sat in dismay.

"You will try to ruin me anyway, Shepherd, what is one more person?" said the judge. He slowly put the knife to her throat and dragged it across her skin. People began to scream as the blood ran from her throat. The judge dropped the knife and ran toward the front door. He pushed aside the people who were waiting for a table as he ran out the front door. The hostess fell to the floor as the blood ran down her neck. Shepherd got up and ran over to her. "Someone call 911," he said.

The manager of the restaurant stood there in a state of shock. Once again, Shepherd yelled, "Call an ambulance, this girl is still alive!" The manager turned and ran for the phone.

Dino, Bill and Jezebel sat there stunned by what just happened. Jezebel got up to see if she could help the poor girl. Just then, two paramedics walked in with a stretcher.

The place was thinning out; many people got up from their tables and left already.

The paramedics yelled, "Please, people, can we make some room here?" Dino watched them as they took the woman's vital signs. Something about them struck Dino as wrong.

They were dressed in white uniforms. He noticed the star tattooed on the backs of their hands. They didn't spend much time on her and immediately lifted her onto the stretcher to take her out to the ambulance that was waiting.

"Does something seem a little funny with those paramedics?" Dino asked Bill.

Bill looked at Dino. "You want to pick apart the paramedics at a time like this?"

"Never mind," said Dino.

They carried the poor girl out, leaving behind only the bloodstained carpet. The police came and began to question everyone. No one could believe that a judge could just go insane like that. The congressman had slipped out the back exit door during all the commotion, not wanting to be involved. The police began questioning Bill about his version of what exactly happened, when Dino got up while puffing on his cigar and said in a deep voice, "I'll tell you what happened, that judge is no judge."

"What do you mean, sir?" asked one of the police officers. "Well, I happen to know he was once my client."

Just then the detective from the police station came over. It was the one who made Jezebel uncomfortable, the one she swore she saw at Doctor Senrab's house.

"Here you are at another crime scene. How do we know that you didn't kill her?"

"Watch it, watch it," said Weiler, "this is my client you're talking to. You have anything to say, detective, you need to talk to me first. You know, if you have any more questions, you should be asking Congressman Shepherd. He was the one who was sitting with the good judge and now just mysteriously disappeared. A little strange, if you ask me."

Dino turned around and saw Jezebel sitting in the booth, crying. "Jez, are you okay?" asked Dino.

"What a horrible thing to watch. I feel so bad for this poor girl," said Jez. Weiler interrupted, "Maybe you ought to get her home, Vicelli."

"You're right," said Dino.

Dino grabbed Jez by the arm, helping her out of the booth. "I'll call you in the morning, Bill."

CHAPTER FOURTEEN

They caught a cab that took them to Dino's house. They felt safer not running from the police anymore.

They started to open the front door, while noticing a business card wedged into the door. The card read, *Meet me at the harbor, pier 39 at 10 P.M. tonight.* He turned the card over, and it was Humberto's card. The little guy who owned the bar he used to frequent before Lackahair was killed.

"Who is that?" asked Jez. He gave the card to her so she could read it, and he went straight to the phone to call Bill Weiler. There was no answer, so he left a message about Humberto's card. It was already 9:10, so Dino figured he had better start making his way to the pier.

"I'll go with you," said Jez.

"No," Dino said. "No, you won't. This is too dangerous. I want you to stay here. Besides, I need to talk to Humberto alone."

He caught a cab that pulled up to the dark, foggy pier; the driver asked Dino, "Would you like me to wait?"

Dino said, "Yeah, that would be a good idea."

It was now 9:55. As Dino was waiting in the back seat of the cab, he looked out on the pier and saw the strange little Chihuahua wearing the large brim hat. He was standing way out at the end of the pier.

Dino got out and walked to the end through the fog. "Hunberto," Dino yelled.

"Vicelli, it is me," he said with his little accent. "I have some information for you, Vicelli."

Dino walked up to him and lit a cigar. It was very cold on the pier, and Dino was glad that he wore his tan overcoat.

Humberto said, "There is something very strange going on in my bar. The man, a tall man, a doctor comes in one day, sits down and orders a drink from my new girl. You know Lackahair, we miss her, such a tragedy." "I know, Humberto, but please, can we move on with this story?" said Dino.

"Oh, sorry, Vicelli, well anyway, a couple minutes later, another man comes in and sits down at the other end of the bar and I couldn't believe my eyes, it was the same man, they looked identical. I thought, you know, maybe this man has a twin, but they weren't sitting together. They have been watching my place every day. I know because they are always around when I close at night and take the garbage out. They stand far away, but I see them with their binoculars."

"What did these men look like?" asked Dino. "Very tall men," said Humberto.

"Well, anyone would be considered tall to you, Humberto," said Dino. "Ha, you're right, Señor. Well, the men wore blue suits, had black hair and olive skin."

"That sounds like Jim Barnes," said Dino.

"Let me tell you, señor, these men did everything alike, their actions, their expressions, everything. I don't get it. Before they left, the man who came in first handed me his business card and said to give it to you. I forgot to bring it, but I read the card, and all it said was, *'You're next, Vicelli.'* It was a blank card except for the writing," said Humberto.

A bullet suddenly ricocheted off the nearby wooden post.

"Get down, it's a setup! They must have followed you here," yelled Dino.

"What," yelled Humberto, as Dino hit the planked floor. Humberto fell into the water, and a flying bullet hit him.

"Humberto, Humberto," Dino yelled, "are you okay, where are you?" Dino heard him fall into the water, but didn't realize he had actually been hit by a bullet. Dino crawled on his belly to the side of the pier, looking over, fearing the worst about Humberto.

There was no sound coming from the water. Dino heard the footsteps coming down the long plank behind him. He knew he was trapped, and he thought of jumping into the water, but they might still be able to kill him.

"Vicelli, nowhere to run."

He lay flat on the pier, face down as he heard the cocking of the gun above his ear.

"Get up," the voice said. Dino slowly got up and turned around, and sure enough, it was the two paramedics who were in the restaurant. They were the two who carried away the dead hostess.

"I didn't think you guys were real paramedics," said Dino as he smirked. They took him by the arms and walked him to the car. They sat Dino in the back seat and started to close the door when Dino kicked one of the men in the leg, pushing the car door open. He hit the other man in the stomach,

knocking him off his feet and causing him to drop the gun.

Dino went for the gun, but the other man kicked the gun away from him; there was a fight to get to the gun. Dino, tried to reach it with his fingers, so close, he thought, so close. The other man fell to the ground, then he got up and grabbed the gun, hitting Dino behind the head and knocking him out. They put him in the car and took him to the doctor's house.

Dino woke up to the sounds of wheels rolling across the floor. He was moving and trying to get up. Everything was very hazy through his eyes. He felt groggy while looking at the lights on the ceiling through hazed, foggy eyes.

His eyelids were so heavy; he kept fighting to keep them open. All of his strength was draining out of him. He tried to move his arms, but couldn't. He looked down and noticed the restraints on his arms. He was on a stretcher. He was being wheeled down a hall to somewhere, but he didn't know where. He then passed out.

He woke up to a glass chamber surrounding him. The beeping noise was a wire attached to his arm. He looked around the room, and there he spotted the redheaded hostess from the restaurant. She was also in a vertical glass case, hanging from the ceiling. He noticed there were no blood marks on her throat. Her body looked as it did before the murder. He felt as though he were in a meat market, waiting for a slaughter.

He put his hands on the top of the glass, trying to push his way out. Then a voice said, "I don't think that's going to get you anywhere, Mr. Vicelli." He could see Jim Barnes standing above him, looking down. Then another Barnes appeared.

Dino knew that this had to be a dream.

"What is going on, Barnes?" asked Dino. Dino's voice was muffled through the glass.

"I'm not Barnes; well, actually, I am in a way. My name is Dr. Senrab." "You are Dr. Senrab?" asked Dino.

"Yes, Barnes is my clone. He was actually the first one that I did. Good likeness, isn't it? Something went wrong with him, though. He is a very nice and caring character, unlike me.

"You see, he doesn't know that he was cloned. Katy Barnes, my colleague's secretary, he was married to her. However, I always thought he was such a handsome man. He was the perfect specimen. She found out that I had cloned him, but I threatened her that if she ever told him or anyone else, she would cease to exist. I actually had her convinced for a while. She told Tyson that she was going to tell Jim. Therefore, you see I had to get rid of her.

"Barnes is such a simple man. I always thought that if I could put his looks with my brains, what a perfect combination. Then I got carried away with making more. If all of my clones are in different places at different times, can you imagine how much we can accomplish? Do you think that he knows that his precious wife is dead, Mr. Vicelli?"

"No, Dr. Senrab, he does not, poor guy. All he wanted was to find his wife, alive!"

"I am curious, how is it that Barnes doesn't realize that he was cloned? I mean, how can you actually clone somebody and them not know it?" asked Vicelli.

"Very simple," said Senrab. "They have no memory after I am finished with them. When I take them, they are under a heavy drug. Mr. Barnes has no clue, and he has never seen me, and I am going to try to keep it like that. Same thing for his wife, Katy; however, I transformed her into the beautiful afghan that she is. When have you ever seen a dog walking around looking like that?"

"You are insane, Senrab. What are your plans for me? I know I must be in this glass case for a reason, and what happened to that poor hostess from the restaurant? I see her body just hanging there. I would also like to know why you had to kill Humberto and Lackahair?"

"I am going to give you the courtesy of answering all of your questions, because you won't remember a thing anyway after this is all over. So let us say that I am doing this out of the goodness of my heart, so to speak.

"If you are referring to the little barmaid at Humberto's, did you know that she was actually an FBI agent? She had been snooping around on my tail for a long time. I had to get rid of her. She was beginning to find out too much. However, the way I look at it, I remade her my way; she will work for me now. Your friend Humberto was just a casualty, unfortunately. I needed him to draw you out to the pier."

"Are you going to clone me as well?" Dino asked him in a joking way, not expecting him to answer in the manner that he did.

"Of course, Mr. Vicelli. Why do you think you are here? With all of your talents as a private eye, and let's not forget your notoriety. I think you are a very smart man, and you have cracked many cases. I could send several of you to Europe to do some work for me and use you here as well. You could play a big part in my operation. I am making the world a better place to live."

"How is that?" asked Dino.

"My way is easier to control people," said Senrab. "You won't get away with this, Senrab."

"And why not, Mr. Vicelli, I have before." "Too many people know where I am." "Oh?" said Senrab, "like who?"

"Well, for one, Jezebel. She knows where you live, and if I don't come back home, this will be the first place she will come looking for me."

"Oh, and Mr. Vicelli, I will be ready for her. Now, I am going to give you a little shot here to make you sleep." Dino began trying to rise up out of the restraints. The more he fought, the tighter the restraints became. He felt something going down past his left shoulder and into his arm. Dino quickly fell into a deep sleep.

He began to dream about several Jezebels running over to him, but he couldn't make out which was the real one. They were each crying and wondering why he didn't recognize them as the real one, each one saying, "Dino, it's me, how come you don't know me?" Dino quickly ran away from them in frustration. He kept running until he came to a very high brick wall. As he looked up, he noticed those long legs dangling down above him.

"Hello, handsome," she said. She jumped straight down off the wall and into his arms.

"Jezebel, is it really you?" he asked.

"Well, who else would it be?" she asked. "Those other ones that look like me, they are just shells. They don't have feelings or emotions like I have."

Then he heard a voice crying from afar, "Dino, Dino." He couldn't recognize the voice, and then it felt as though something were drawing him away from Jezebel. He felt the pulling on him so strongly that he dropped Jezebel, feeling himself lifted off his feet. The suction was very forceful. He didn't know what was happening to him. Two arms extended around his waist. He turned around, and it was Lackahair.

"Oh, Lackahair," he shouted with surprise, "I thought you were dead.

How is it that you're here? I don't understand."

"Dino," she said, "don't try. I can't explain anything to you, but the most important thing is that we are together again. I will never leave you again."

Then he looked in front of him, and Dr. Senrab was pulling Jezebel by the hair to one of the clone chambers. She was screaming and trying to fight him off, but couldn't.

"Jezebel, no, don't let him do this to you," yelled Dino.

Meanwhile, Lackahair would not let go of Dino, telling him to let Jezebel go. She was reassuring him that the doctor knows what he is doing and not to interfere. Jezebel was crying out to Dino. Dino was so confused.

He watched as Jezebel was stuffed into the chamber. He then watched as her whole body lit up like a Christmas tree. Senrab started pulling switches on the wall, and the show began. All of her beautiful hair had disappeared; her skeletal features would appear as her skin disappeared. He looked over at the chamber next to her, and the same thing was happening to a woman, a tall, beautiful blonde-haired woman. On the front of the encasement, it read *"KATY BARNES."*

Dino felt helpless. The more he tried to pull away from Lackahair, the tighter her grip became. He wanted so badly to help Jezebel and couldn't.

He closed his eyes; he couldn't watch any more of this madness. Then when he opened his eyes, the bodies in the encasements had switched places. He looked over at the four other encasements, and they all looked like Jezebel. Dino figured out that the doctor needed the first person he had cloned to make additional clones. Even though that person might be dead, he froze their cells and their bodies and used them repeatedly to make new specimens.

Then he felt sharp claws go into his ribs. The pain was excruciating as he gasped.

"You're next," said Lackahair.

"It was you who wrote on the back of the card that Humberto was telling me about." Dino wondered what happened to the sweet, wonderful girl that he used to know. She pushed him closer to the encasements as they were taking Katy Barnes out. He then saw all of the Jezebels rise and climb out of the cases and walked away.

"Pretty amazing, isn't it, Mr. Vicelli?" Senrab asked. "No one will ever be as clever as I am. I have big plans for this world," as he laughed boisterously. "You can come closer, Vicelli, it won't hurt that bad," he said with his sinister laugh.

Then Dino woke up and he realized he had been dreaming. The front doorbell was ringing. It took him a minute to realize where he was.

Senrab told his assistant to find out who was at the door. The assistant came back down and said, "It is the police, with Vicelli's attorney. He gave me his card. I think that you had better talk to him, Dr. Senrab."

Senrab opened the door and asked, "What can I do for you gentlemen?" "Well," said Bill Weiler, "we are looking for him," as he showed a picture of Dino.

"Can't help you, don't really know who he is." "Are you sure, Doctor Senrab?" Mr. Weiler asked. "Yes, I am, gentlemen," said Senrab.

Jezebel came up behind Bill Weiler. "He didn't come back to the house last night. Doctor, I know he is in there," she said.

"We do have a search warrant, doctor, so if you would kindly step aside," the police officer said.

Bill Weiler kept studying Senrab, as Senrab asked, "Is something wrong?"

"Well, it's uncanny, you look identical to a judge I know, who is actually wanted for questioning regarding a murder."

"Well, you know," said Senrab, "in today's world, there are many people who look like other people."

"Well, not this much of a striking resemblance," said Weiler. They pushed the doctor out of the way and proceeded downstairs.

"Dino, are you here? I think I know where he might be," Jezebel yelled. She led them down to the laboratory. They ran over to the case by the wall where Dino was. They pulled Senrab down the stairs to open the case to let Dino out. Senrab pushed a button on the wall and opened the case, and Dino climbed out very slowly, still feeling a little drugged and tired.

"Thank God you are all right," she said. Weiler asked, "Are you okay, Dino?" Dino replied, "I think so."

"I was a little leery when I got that message from you, Vicelli, about Humberto. Poor guy, we found him dead when we got to the pier. He was floating on top of the water," said Weiler.

Weiler and the police looked around at all the strange cases and equipment. "What is all this, Senrab?" asked Weiler. "Is this a laboratory or something?"

"Hey, officers, look, there is the hostess that was just killed at the Contempt of Court restaurant," said Weiler.

"You're under arrest, Dr. Senrab, for kidnapping and murder. By the way, cloning is against the law as well, in case you didn't know it."

Weiler looked at the officer and said, "Well, I guess you found the real killer of that FBI agent, and as far as the killing of Jezebel Collins, here she is alive and well. This puts my client in the clear."

They turned to Senrab. "Did you have anything to do with Humberto's death?" asked Weiler.

"No," said Senrab. As he was talking, he was backing up to the credenza, where he happened to have a gun stashed in the drawer.

He backed up very slowly so that no one would notice what he was doing. One of the officers was eyeing him very carefully.

"So why do you think that I would have anything to do with his murder?" Senrab asked as he reached into the drawer, pulled out the gun and said, "Everyone stay right where you are."

"Wait a minute, Senrab, the place is surrounded with police. You won't be able to go too far."

He pointed the gun toward Jezebel, "Come over here, my dear, you are going with me. You are my insurance."

She grabbed Dino's hand and clenched it, saying, "No, I won't go with you." He then pointed the gun at Dino. "Well, then I am just going to have to shoot your friend here."

"Okay," she said. "I'll go." She walked over to Senrab, and he grabbed her by the arm as they climbed the stairs.

They started to walk out the front door, and a shot was fired past Senrab's left ear.

"I'll kill her if you shoot again," he yelled. One man yelled, "Hold your fire."

Jezebel's arm felt as though it were about to break off, as his grip was so tight.

"You are hurting me, doctor," she said.

He didn't answer her. He quickly made his way across the grass toward the garage where his car was. Then all of a sudden the sprinklers came on, and Jezebel screamed and jumped.

Senrab lost his grip on her and dropped the gun. Jezebel crawled across the grass very quickly until she could get her momentum up to run. Senrab was fumbling through the grass for his gun, when six police officers surrounded him with their guns drawn on him. They put handcuffs on him, reading him his rights. He turned back and saw all of his assistants handcuffed and brought out of the house.

Jezebel looked up and saw Dino coming out of the house, and she ran to him. Weiler helped Dino into his car.

CHAPTER FIFTEEN

The police car pulled up in front of the jailhouse as Dr. Senrab stepped out of the back seat to cameras flashing and reporters throwing all sorts of questions at him. The tall, good-looking doctor remained very calm and confident.

"I'm sure that our great and wonderful police department will be made well aware of the mistake they have made by arresting me, which by the way will be a big lawsuit from me. I am innocent, and that will come out." They hustled him through the crowd quickly to quiet him down.

While he walked into the station, all eyes were upon him. The news was out all over about the sinister doctor's arrest. He walked by his detective friend, whom he knew, and they nodded at each other. Then he was fingerprinted and put into a cell.

Dino returned home with Jezebel, feeling very weak and tired as he walked through the front door and over to the couch where he lay down.

"You know," he said, "I don't even know how long I was gone or how long I was in that chamber. I feel very drugged still. I just don't feel like myself."

"Well, just who do you feel like," laughed Jez.

"No, really Jez, I think there is something wrong with me."

"Oh, sugar," she said, "you are home safe now with me, so there is nothing to worry your handsome little head about."

"Would you please give me a cigar in my top drawer?" he asked. "Sure," she said.

She walked over and opened the top drawer, and there were no cigars. She looked through the drawers below and still couldn't find the cigars; in fact, all of his drawers were empty. She yelled to him, "Dino, sweetheart, your drawers are all empty."

"What?" he yelled. "That is impossible. I had a whole box of Cubans in there, which I just bought from Bud's."

"I am telling you, sugar, there is nothing in these drawers at all." Dino went over to the drawers and saw that they were indeed empty.

"Someone has taken my clothes."

He went to his closet, and the clothes were also gone.

"Now why would someone want my clothes? Even my shoes are gone." Dino searched the rest of the house, and there was nothing else missing except his clothes.

Just then, he heard a noise outside, like someone walking past the window. He went over to the window and there was the spitting image of him, same build, same height, carrying a pile of clothes and shoes thrown over his shoulder and the Cuban cigars in his hand.

Dino opened the window and yelled, "Hey, come back here with my things."

"Jezebel," he said, "get me a flashlight."

Dino ran to the front door as Jezebel handed him the flashlight. The dog in the yard turned around, and the light caught his face.

"Oh no, it's me," said Dino.

He looked at Dino with a stunned look as he paused. His eyes opened so wide that you could see the total whites of the eye.

"Ahh, Buddy, you can buy more clothes," he said as he tiptoed across the grass very quickly.

Dino kept yelling, "Hey, who are you?"

Dino ran out of the front door as he saw him get into a cab and drive off. "Oh, Dino, that could have been your twin," said Jez.

"I know, why did he take all of my clothes? Did he leave me anything?" asked Dino.

They both searched through the closets and drawers, and there was nothing left, except for the white shirt and black pants that Dino was wearing and his black soft-soled shoes. They were both extremely confused, not knowing what to think.

Dino picked up the phone and called Bill Weiler. Bill answered the phone in a rather groggy tone of voice.

"Hello," he said.

"Bill, I just saw someone that looked identical to me."

"What?" said Bill. "Do you know what time it is, Vicelli? Couldn't this have waited until morning? It is 11:30 at night."

"Yeah, I know, Bill, but I couldn't believe what I just saw. I think I have a twin running around who happens to like my clothes."

"Vicelli, I think it might be the drugs you are on that are making you hallucinate."

"Yeah, seriously, he was just in my house, I saw him leaving, and I felt as though I was looking in the mirror. He is a thief. We need to find out where this guy came from," said Dino.

"Well, I'll pay a visit to the jail tomorrow to have a little chat with our Dr. Senrab. Nevertheless, as for right now, I'm going back to sleep," said Weiler.

"Sorry, Bill, didn't mean to wake you," said Dino.

Dino turned to Jez and said, "I want to go to Senrab's house tomorrow, since he won't be there. If we can find his cloning formula, we can destroy it and he will never be able to do this again."

"Isn't that a little dangerous, I mean, what if he comes home?" she asked. "Ya know, Jez, something is really bothering me."

"What is?" she asked.

"Well, suppose that the cloning effort really did go through on me." "Oh, Dino, I seriously doubt that," she said.

"Well, then, why did that guy look so much like me?"

"Honestly, Dino, do you know how many people they say have other people who look so much like them? Besides, it was so dark you really don't know if he looked exactly like you."

"Yeah, I guess you are right," he said.

*　　*　　*

They drove to Dr. Senrab's house, which was surrounded by yellow tape put there by the police.

"Let's ring the doorbell first and make sure the house is empty. I think that we should start with the upstairs bedroom and work our way down to the basement," said Dino.

When no one answered the door, they climbed through an unlocked window.

Just then, Dino's cell phone rang. "Vicelli," he said.

"Vicelli, Bill Weiler here, we have a little problem. It seems as though Dr. Senrab may be getting out on bail."

"What? This is a murder charge."

"Yeah, well, he has the money to make bail, that is for sure. I will keep you posted," said Weiler.

Dino hung up and turned to Jez. "That was Bill; apparently, Senrab is getting out on bail. We had better wrap it up here."

"Why don't we go down to the basement first before we leave; after all," said Jez, "it's not as though he is coming directly home this minute. I think we have a little time. Now is our chance to see how everything really operates down there, since no one is around to interrupt us."

"All right" said Dino. As they started downstairs, they noticed a set of bookshelves in the wall. On the shelves were books on animal behavior, human psychology, human anatomy, and many other scientific books. All the books were lined up very neatly side by side except for one, titled *THE SCIENCE OF CLONING THE PERFECT HUMAN BEING*. That particular book was lying on its side, face down. Dino picked up the book and began to thumb through it. As he did so, three notebook papers folded very neatly fell to the floor. He bent down to pick up the papers and noticed all kind of formulas, along with all different names of cloned people. Looking through the names, he noticed some who were government officials.

He put the papers in his pocket, and they went down the stairs to the long corridor leading to the laboratory. As they started to get closer to the lab, they noticed the lights flickering.

"Dino, look," said Jez. "I think someone may be here."

"No," said Dino, "I seriously doubt it, they closed this place, you know that. If it weren't for that window being slightly open, we would-n't have gotten in."

They opened the lab doors; there stood the other Dino staring him right in the eyes. He looked to the left of his twin. There was Senrab, standing there laughing.

"Well, look who it is," said Senrab. "It's your clone," as he looked at the Dino standing beside him. The real Dino was in shock. He just stood there, unable to speak, staring at him.

"I would have never believed it if I hadn't seen it with my own eyes. Are you okay, Dino?" asked Jez.

"Who are you? Moreover, why do you have my clothes on?" asked Dino.

He walked slowly over to his clone, and with each step, Dino's eyes moved slowly up and down this creature as he was looking for something that wasn't identical to him. He walked slowly around the clone, looking down at his feet and slowly working his way up. Dino put his hands on the clone's shoulders to see if he felt the same as himself. Then he looked up at Senrab, saying, "How did you get out of jail so quickly?"

"I didn't, Vicelli, I have been here all along. I never left my house. My clone did, however, he will do my time for me, and I can just stay here doing more cloning and doing the thing that I was created to do," said Senrab.

"I did a nice job on you, didn't I?" asked Senrab. "You can't find one flaw, can you?"

"Why me?" asked Vicelli.

"Well," said Senrab, "you have such an inquisitive nature and a great deal of intelligence. I can have him do the things that I want him to do. See, I don't think you're as dishonest as I would like you to be. I can mold him into what I want. There is a lot of work to do in this world and a lot of information that I need, and I know you would not get it for me, so I created another you. He even sounds like you. I have not perfected the cigar smoking yet. Say something, Vicelli number two."

"My name is Vicelli," he said.

"Oh, my, Dino," said Jez, "he does sound like you." "You will never get away with this, Senrab," said Dino.

"Oh, but I'm afraid I will," said Senrab, "that is where you are wrong.

No one will be able to tell the difference, besides us." "I will go to the police," said Dino.

"Mr. Vicelli, if you went to the police with this story, they would put you in a place for the mentally insane. No one would ever believe you," said Senrab.

Just then, Senrab grabbed a cigar and put it into the mouth of the clone.

The clone began to cough and gag and then vomited. "Oh, well, we will have to practice," said Senrab. Dino looked at Jez with disgust.

"Come on, Dino, I think we should go," she said. "But, Jez, I need to stop him" said Dino.

"You're not going to stop me, Vicelli," said Senrab.

"Well you can bet that I will be back with the police," said Dino.

"Go ahead, they won't find anything here, we will be long gone. My clone will be out on bail soon, and the police will think it's life as usual. He will come back here to the house and no one will know the difference."

"How did you do it? Senrab, how did you make the switch when the police were taking you into custody?"

"Oh, Vicelli, I could never tell you that. I wouldn't want you to know how I operate."

"I will be watching you, Senrab, so if I were you I would watch your step. Come on, Jezebel," he said as he grabbed her hand, turned, and walked back down the long corridor and up the stairs to the front door.

Just then, there was a loud explosion. The whole house shook and debris began falling from the ceiling. They turned around and saw a cloud of smoke following them up the stairs and then another explosion. This time, fire was chasing them.

They ran up the stairs and toward the door at the top, and it was locked. They frantically banged on the door, trying to get out. They kept trying the doorknob and it wouldn't budge. They couldn't get out.

Jezebel began to scream, "Dino, we can't get out. We are going to die." "No, Jezebel, get a hold of yourself." They both began choking and coughing. Through the flames that were getting very close to them, he could see an axe at the bottom of the stairs. The flames were beginning to engulf them as breathing became more difficult.

"Dino, you will never make it down the stairs," said Jezebel.

By this time, the flames were still at the bottom of the stairs, but the smoke was very thick and heavy. They both began pushing on the door together, hoping that the weight would force the door open. Dino turned and ran down the stairs, covering his face with his hands, feeling the heat penetrating his skin like hot coals. He saw the axe, picked it up, ran quickly up the stairs, and began to chop a hole in the door.

The axe was so large and heavy that Dino had a rough time lifting it. He dragged it up the stairs. He chopped away until there was a hole large enough to climb through to the other side. The flames were climbing quickly up the stairs behind them. Jezebel climbed through first; panicking with every breath she took. Dino followed her as she was screaming at him, "Hurry up." Dino could feel the flames crowding behind him as he made his way through the door. At this point, he could feel the heat warming his skin.

They ran to the main door and quickly ran out onto the front grass. They were gasping for air and choking as they fell to the ground.

Just then, there was another explosion as they watched the roof blow off the laboratory. Then the whole house went up into flames. They both lay on the grass, gasping for air. Then the fire trucks began to arrive.

"Are you all right?" yelled one of the firemen as they approached Dino and Jez.

"Yes, I just need to catch my breath. What an awful experience," she said with her southern drawl.

"Oh, Dino," she added, "this means that your clone and that awful man are dead. I wonder what caused the explosion."

The firefighters began hosing down the intense flames of the fire. They turned to Dino, asking, "Was there anyone else in there?"

"No," said Dino, "the house was empty."

Jez looked at him as if to say, smart thinking. Dino knew that the police did not know about Dr. Senrab's clone, or for that matter, Dino's clone, so they wouldn't ever be missed.

They picked themselves up off the grass and began to walk away from the awful scene of the fire.

Just then, the clone of Dr. Senrab drove up and began walking over to Dino and Jezebel.

"Well, Mr. Vicelli, what did you do this time, burn down my house?" "No, Senrab, I did not burn your house down. I really don't know what happened. I do, however, know who you really are. I think we both know that, don't we, Senrab?"

"I really don't have a clue as to what you are talking about," said Senrab. A detective came over from the police department.

"There will be a full investigation on the fire. It is too bad this happened, Dr. Senrab."

Dino and Jezebel walked away with their torn clothes and the smell of smoke on them. They turned and looked back, wondering what would become of Senrab's clone and if it was really Senrab's clone. Could it be that the clone burned in the fire and the person standing on the front lawn was the real Senrab, or was it Jim Barnes? This they would never know.

T H E   E N D

www.ingramcontent.com/pod-product-compliance
Lightning Source LLC
Chambersburg PA
CBHW032020180726
48283CB00008B/2761